Dear Reader,

Have you ever been tempted to do something that is totally wrong for you? What is it about a taboo that makes breaking all the rules so seductive? Why is it that people will often risk destruction pursuing the very thing they shouldn't have?

These were the thematic questions that circled my head as I sat down to write *High Stakes Seduction.* Because you see, Adam Mancuso is a highly disciplined naval special security agent and he's been tasked with staking out the ex-girlfriend of someone suspected of stealing top secret information. There's only one problem. Eva St. George is the sexiest woman Adam has ever laid eyes on.

Adam has always prided himself on his self-discipline and high moral principles, but he never counted on someone like Eva tempting him. Is Eva a spy? Is her seduction calculated to drive him wild? Or is she just a sexy woman who's stirred his blood and captured his heart like no other?

I hope you enjoy reading about Adam and Eva's sizzling romance. And please, tell all your friends about the wonderful, heart-warming, uplifting, romantic stories they can find between the covers of Harlequin books.

Lori Wilde

Lori Wilde

HIGH STAKES SEDUCTION

TORONTO NEW YORK LONDON
AMSTERDAM PARIS SYDNEY HAMBURG
STOCKHOLM ATHENS TOKYO MILAN MADRID
PRAGUE WARSAW BUDAPEST AUCKLAND

Recycling programs
for this product may
not exist in your area.

ISBN-13: 978-0-373-79614-4

HIGH STAKES SEDUCTION

Copyright © 2011 by Laurie Vanzura

ABOUT THE AUTHOR

Lori Wilde is the author of forty books. She's been nominated for a RITA® Award and four *RT Book Reviews* Reviewers' Choice Awards. Her books have been excerpted in *Cosmopolitan, Redbook* and *Quick & Simple.* Lori teaches writing online through Ed2go. She's also an R.N. trained in forensics, and she volunteers at a women's shelter. Visit her website at www.loriwilde.com.

Books by Lori Wilde

To all the lovely ladies of the VIP lounge. You rock!

1

NAKED YOGA?

Navy Special Security Officer Lieutenant Adam Mancuso pressed his eyes to the state-of-the-art, wide-angle binocular-telescope mounted on a tripod. He frowned in stern disapproval while at the same time his pulse kicked up.

His target was doing yoga in the nude.

Warrior Pose, if he wasn't mistaken.

He had no business staring at the woman once he realized what she was doing. His surveillance assignment was limited to her comings and goings and those of her guests. He was violating her privacy. She had a right to do naked yoga in her own living room if she chose.

Never mind that she hadn't quite pulled the drapes all the way closed. With this kick-ass telescope he could spot a fly in a sandstorm from two miles away.

And he could see every incredible detail of Eva St. George's lush, supple body. Those pert breasts, narrow waist, lean legs and luscious, luscious ass.

Fascination dried his saliva. Lust drained the blood from his face and drove it straight to his dick.

Move, dammit. Step away from the telescope.

Transfixed, he fisted his hands and clenched his jaw.

He was going to stop this. Right now. Except who could move with a boner the size of Catalina?

Shake it off, Mancuso.

How could he, when such a glorious sight met his eyes? Right, that was nothing but an excuse. He hated what he was doing. Totally disgusted with his caveman behavior. And yet, he did not move.

He was caught off guard. Knocked for a loop. Who would have expected the woman to strip off all her clothing and jump into the lotus position without any warning? He was too rattled to even blink, much less take a step back from the telescope.

Neanderthal. Troglodyte. Ape.

Yeah, sure, calling himself names would work. His toes curled inside his boots anchored on the hardwood floors of the rented apartment in San Diego. His eyes were practically bugging out of their sockets as he watched the oh-so-perky Ms. St. George do something with her body he hadn't thought humanly possible.

Her skin glistened with perspiration, her adorable blond ponytail swishing as she moved. *Hi Ho, Silver.* He licked his lips gone Sahara desert dry. Man alive, it was hot in here in spite of the breeze blowing in through the open window, bringing with it the smell of the Pacific Ocean and rustling the curtains.

Here she was stretching and bending and twisting, naked as the day she was born, without a clue that she was being watched. She thought she was safe in her own home, protected from prying eyes. Free to express herself with that body bestowed by the gods. She had no idea that she was under scrutiny by the U.S. Navy.

That thought got through to him when nothing else had. He could not afford to forget why he was here or whom he represented. Military secrets had been stolen and if they fell into the wrong hands American lives would be in jeopardy.

Then she turned and he spotted something on her left shoulder that seemed to flitter in the flickering glow from the candles she'd lighted before starting her erotic exercise. Something silvery and blue. He fiddled with the focus, honing in on it.

A tattoo.

Of a handsome blue-and-silver butterfly, wings unfurling, ready to fly free.

He should have figured. Everything in her dossier pointed to a free-spirited, no-regrets type. That made her his polar opposite in every way. According to her file, St. George had grown up without a father and trailing after her nomadic, hairstylist mother from town to town.

Adam had been raised as the oldest of three kids in a stable, well-to-do military family that set the bar high. His father had also served in the Navy and upon his retirement, had followed the family tradition of going into politics. Adam was expected to follow suit, marry a woman who could navigate that world with ease and aplomb, all the while exhibiting the highest moral conduct.

And yet, here you are staring at a naked woman through a telescope.

She stretched to the side, giving him a perfect view of the butterfly. Body art had never turned him on before, but something about *that* tattoo on *this* woman stirred an unexpected reaction inside him.

Sweat broke out on his brow and he sank his top teeth into his bottom lip, suppressing a groan.

She dropped like silk panties to the floor, pressing her belly down flat on the yoga mat stretched over the hardwood flooring, while at the same time angling her fantastic butt into the air.

Holy crap! What was this new pose? The erection that had already been straining against his zipper tightened and grew. His blood ran red-hot through his veins and his breath shot out in quick, hard rasps.

The bottom of her ponytail grazed the middle of her back just above where her sexy little waist tucked inward. She arched her spine, shifting her position again, putting that impressive little fanny right in his face.

His throat constricted. The muscles of her sweet ass were tightly defined, but at the same time utterly feminine. His gaze tracked from the curvy rump to where it joined her thighs that tapered down into long shapely legs. Her peachy skin glistened with the glossy sheen of exertion. Adam wanted to touch her so badly his hands shook. A woman like that could lead a good man straight to hell with a big grin on his face.

Gotta stop this. Gotta stop this now.

Otherwise he was going to unzip his pants and do what came naturally.

No. No way. No how. He was known throughout the Office of Naval Intelligence for his self-control. He wasn't about to jack off over the woman he'd been hired to keep under surveillance. That would be unethical and sleazy and…and…

He closed his eyes, took a deep breath, straightened and finally stepped back from the telescope. He paced the floor, ran a hand over his close-cropped hair, and took several deep breaths to calm his soaring temperature.

If she was going to put on that kind of floor show every night, Adam didn't know if he'd survive this assignment. Maybe he could ask Rogers to take the night shift—

No!

The minute the thought entered his mind he squelched it. The only thing worse than having to watch her nude yoga routine was the thought of his partner watching her. Never mind that Tim Rogers had just gotten married and was madly in love with his new bride. Adam didn't want the other Naval Intelligence officer ogling Eva.

And why the hell was that?

Adam surely didn't know. It was a strange, possessive feeling gnawing at his gut. He didn't want anyone seeing her naked but him.

It shocked him. That sudden thought.

The door to the apartment opened and Adam jumped in front of the telescope, arms behind his back, guilt punching him. Tim Rogers came through the door carrying a greasy white paper bag that smelled of sautéed onions and two foam drink cups cradled against his body.

Rogers could have posed for a Navy recruitment poster. Tall, dark eyes, hawkish nose. He possessed a wide, welcoming smile and dark brown hair that he wore slightly longer than Adam's but still short enough to meet military regulations. Rogers shot him a sly glance. "How's the peep show?"

"P-peep show?" Adam stammered and felt the top of his ears burn.

"Don't get offended. I know you're Mr. Straight Arrow," his partner said, clearly misreading Adam's embarrassment as disapproval. "But come on, we *are* playing peep-eye with a beautiful woman. Sooner or later, we're going to see her partially dressed if not completely naked." His grin widened. "Perks of the job."

You have no idea, Adam thought, the image of Eva's sexy bare body vividly fresh in his mind.

"Have you told Lisa about our assignment?" Adam asked, shifting the conversation off the woman next door and on to Rogers.

"Do I look like a crazy man?" Rogers chuckled. "I told her I couldn't discuss the case, which is true." He rifled through the sack, pulled out a foam container. "Here's your rabbit food."

Rogers shoved the container into Adam's hand, and then went back to the sack to retrieve a hamburger dripping with grease.

"How do you eat that stuff?" Adam shook his head, reached for a plastic fork to dig into his garden salad with low-cal dressing.

Rogers sank his teeth into the burger. "With relish. Not all of us grew up with a gourmet chef at our beck and call."

"You exaggerate. My family had a cook and housekeeper, not a gourmet chef."

Roger held up a French fry. "Still, not the norm. Wanna bite? I'll share."

"No thanks." Adam had given up eating fast food a long time ago. A disciplined man controlled himself in the face of temptation. No matter how delicious.

And then he thought of Eva St. George again. Talk about temptation of a wholly different kind.

"So," Rogers said, dabbing at his mouth with a napkin. "What do you think we did to piss off the-powers-that-be?"

"What do you mean?" Adam frowned.

"This is just lame babysitting duty. I mean, c'mon, if you were Barksdale would you come dragging back to your ex-girlfriend if *you'd* stolen the prototype to the Navy's newest cutting-edge stealth weapon? Me? I'd get the hell out of the country ASAP."

Keith Barksdale had been a civilian ONI computer analyst in San Diego. While Adam had been working to encrypt the top secret military documents in his office in Suitland, Maryland, Barksdale had remotely hacked into the Navy's computer and stolen the file before Adam had even had a chance to realize what was happening and raise the alarm.

It had taken him and his team almost half an hour to discover where the invader had come from. Once they'd tracked the hacker to San Diego, the local ONI and Naval Criminal Investigative Service had run checks on all the employees who could have been potentially involved in the theft. They'd instantly red-flagged Barksdale when they learned he'd been taking a yoga class with a foreign national who had ties to a country bent on an arms race with the U.S.—and that he owed several hundred thousand dollars in gambling debts.

Barksdale had been taken in for questioning but they'd been unable to prove his involvement—he'd been an expert at covering his tracks—and they'd been forced to release him. The Navy kept him under close surveillance, restricting his computer access and monitoring his every movement, but then the slippery Barksdale had absconded and no one had seen him for three weeks.

The ONI believed he had downloaded the information to a microchip, but that he hadn't yet passed it to his contact. For one thing, there had been no large deposits in Barksdale's bank account before they'd frozen it. For another thing, the suspected buyer was still in the country and taking yoga classes at Miss St. George's studio.

Adam knew exactly why he'd been given the assignment. Even though he'd followed every security protocol to the letter, Barksdale had taken it right out from under his nose and the Navy was highly embarrassed. This was his chance to make amends.

"They're just covering all the bases," Adam said mildly. "At least we didn't get the chore of staking out Barksdale's grandmother in her Iowa nursing home."

Rogers gave an exaggerated shudder. "Yeah, you've got a point. But how come we didn't get a more active assignment, like shadowing Barksdale's contact?"

"This is an active assignment."

"Uh-huh." Rogers took a long swing from his drink. "Keep telling yourself that. Higgins put his glory boy Kilgore on the buyer," he said, referring to their commander, George Higgins, and their nemesis, Miles Kilgore, who seemed to get all the plum assignments.

"Higgins called it as he saw fit," Adam replied. "Barksdale could very well contact Ms. St. George. We've got the heat on him hard. He'll have trouble getting out of the country or even finding a safe house. It's natural to assume he could turn to her for help."

"Would you go to your ex-girlfriend if you were in trouble?"

He thought about Kirsten, the woman he'd almost married. They'd been so much alike. She was dutiful, dedicated, calm and controlled. It was that self-control that had torpedoed their relationship. She'd broken things off after three years, telling him she needed someone who stirred her passion. *That* had been a kick in the teeth.

Adam winced at the memory. It would be difficult, but sure, yeah, if he were in trouble he'd go to Kirsten. They might not have had a grand passion, but they had mutual respect and admiration. He shrugged. "Depends on the girlfriend I suppose."

"You don't think Barksdale is smart enough to figure out that we'd have all his family and friends under surveillance? The assignment's lame and you know it. In the meantime, I'm a newlywed stuck clear across the country from my bride."

"Comes with the territory." Adam gave him no sympathy. "You knew what you were getting into when you joined the military." Duty to country often came before family. It was the nature of the beast. He'd had that drilled into him from toddlerhood.

"Well," Rogers said, crumpling up the paper bag and tossing it into the trash can. "I'm hitting the sack. Have a good night."

They ran two surveillance shifts. Rogers kept watch from 7:00 a.m. to 7:00 p.m. Adam had drawn the short straw and pulled the night shift. Now that he saw what Eva did with her late evenings, he was glad.

Rogers yawned, stretched and ambled toward the back of the two-bedroom apartment. The place was barely furnished. The small dining area held two camp chairs and a folding table. In the living room there was a couch and their surveillance equipment—wires, cameras, cords, telescopes, recorders and listening devices. In the bedrooms, twin-size mattresses lay on the floor.

They were stuck here until the assignment was over. How long it lasted depended on how long it took the ONI to apprehend Keith Barksdale. Unless something more pressing happened and the brass decided it wasn't worth the money or manpower keeping tabs on St. George.

Adam went back to the telescope, but Eva was no longer in her living room. She'd blown out the candles and the light was now on in her bedroom. Disappointment settled over him and he realized he'd been hoping to see her naked again.

"Pervert," he chastised himself.

He kept watching, imaging her getting ready for bed, taking a steamy shower, blow-drying her hair, brushing her teeth. He saw the light in her bedroom wink out, envisioned her sinking that slinky body of hers underneath the sheets.

A rush of heat spread through his groin.

Dammit. This had to stop. He had to find a way to turn off his desires. Otherwise he didn't know how long he could stay honorable.

And Adam Mancuso was nothing if not an honorable man.

2

WHENEVER EVA ST. GEORGE got the blues she pulled the drapes, put Enya on the iPod, lit aromatherapy candles, shimmied out of her clothes and let yoga whisk her away.

And today, she was bluer than blue.

It was her twenty-ninth birthday and no one had remembered, but honestly, the funk had really started three weeks ago when her boyfriend, Keith Barksdale, had ditched her.

She didn't know why she was letting Keith get to her. Their relationship hadn't been serious. Most likely it was because he'd dumped her before she had a chance to dump him. It was the first time Eva had ever been on the receiving end of a breakup.

The whole thing had gone down really weirdly. Keith had shown up at her yoga studio one morning and given her a beautiful platinum locket clearly worth a lot of money. "I've been thinking of you," he'd said, "and wanted to get you something really nice."

She'd been touched. It was the first time in two months of dating that he'd bought her a gift. Then he'd disappeared for a couple of days and when he returned, he told her that he was breaking things off, that he'd realized they weren't a good match and he wanted the locket back. She'd agreed to return it, but at that moment a black SUV had pulled up in the parking lot. Three men in dark suits and sunglasses had gotten out.

Keith had taken one look at them through the big picture window of her studio, paled considerably and run out the back door. The men had come in, flashed badges and identified themselves as NCIS and asked her to answer a few questions about Keith.

She'd had nothing to hide, so she'd agreed to an interview and told the truth. She had no idea where Keith had gone when he left the yoga studio and she didn't expect to ever hear from him again. It had been disconcerting, however, to learn he'd been involved in some kind of illegal activities. They wouldn't give her details of course, but just knowing Keith was capable of such things put *her* judgment in question.

What was it about her that attracted irresponsible—and sometimes even somewhat shifty—guys? Eva pondered this while she brushed her teeth and stared solemnly into the mirror.

She took stock of herself. She wasn't bad looking, but not gorgeous by any means, although she did keep her body in shape. Her thighs were on the bulky side. Her hair grew too low on her forehead so she had no choice but to wear bangs. She had a small gap between her teeth she could whistle through and a sprinkling of freckles over the bridge of her nose from being dumb about sunscreen when she was a teen.

Sighing, she dipped her head to rinse and caught a glimpse of the tattoo on her shoulder. She'd gotten it during a girls' night out several years ago and while she didn't regret it, she wondered if the tattoo had somehow branded her as a woman who was up for anything. If she were being honest, she'd have to admit that she did like to have a good time. Life was short, right? Why waste your youth? Was *that* why she drew bad boys to her?

But now, with thirty looming in her not too distant future, Eva had to ask herself if it was time to give up her footloose ways. The only thing in her life that kept her anchored was her yoga studio. Until now, it had been enough, but without any warning she felt empty and aimless.

Tonight, however, the yoga hadn't helped. The endorphin rush she usually experienced had eluded her. Instead, she felt drained, numb, weary to the bone and strangely detached. As if she was standing in a long corridor filled with closed doors, unable to make a choice about which one to open and walk through.

Just waiting…waiting… For what, she did not know.

You're just feeling sorry for yourself because no one remembered your birthday. Shake it off.

She finished up in the bathroom, slipped into pajamas and got into bed. "Happy birthday, Eva," she murmured, and turned off the lamp.

It wasn't the worst birthday she'd ever had. After all, she'd treated herself to her favorite Thai takeout. The honor of worst birthday was reserved for her seventh when she and her mom had been living out of their van in Tucson and her mother had stuck a candle in a stale Twinkie and called it a birthday cake.

Eva had started to cry because she'd really wanted a strawberry ice cream cake and she'd accidentally knocked the Twinkie—complete with the lit candle in the shape of the number 7—onto the floor of the van and the icky old carpet had burst into flames.

Angie had dragged her into the convenience store

where she'd bought the Twinkie and the candle, yelling that her house was on fire. Eva remembered being so embarrassed by that. A van *was not* a house.

The fire department arrived with sirens blaring and doused the van. One of the firefighters and Angie had started an affair and he had moved Eva and her mother into a little apartment over a sandwich shop. The shop-keeper gave them the leftover sandwiches at the end of the night. Fried baloney with mayonnaise had been her favorite.

Everything was going good for a change. Then the firefighter's wife had shown up a few weeks later, brandishing a gun and threatening to shoot Angie, until she saw Eva cowering behind her mother and put the weapon away.

Ah, good times.

The truly sad thing was that the firefighter had been one of Angie's better hook-ups.

No sooner had Eva slipped underneath the covers than her phone rang. She propped up on one elbow and peered at the caller ID in the darkness.

It was her half sister Sienna.

Someone had remembered her birthday after all. Smiling, she snagged the cordless phone from its dock and sat up against the headboard. "Hello?"

"Eva! Guess what?" Sienna exclaimed.

The hollow feeling returned to the pit of her stomach. Sienna wasn't calling to wish her a happy birthday. "It must be something big, you sound really excited."

"Ryan popped the question. We're getting married!"

Stunned, Eva couldn't speak.

"Sis? You still there?" Sienna asked breathlessly.

"Um…" She didn't know what to say. Sienna was

only twenty and in her junior year of nursing school. "I'm here."

"You don't sound excited for me."

"I...I didn't realize you and Ryan were that serious," she said, when what she wanted to say was, "Bunny rabbits and kittens, Sienna, you're only twenty, you have the rest of your life to get married."

"He's my soul mate." Sienna sighed dreamily.

"Ryan is the only guy you've ever dated."

"Doesn't matter. When it's right it's right. And it's kind of nice that neither of us has ever been with anyone else. It makes our relationship special."

Yeah, like people who weren't virgins when they hooked up could never have anything special. Eva bit her tongue.

"Besides, we *have* been dating for four years."

"I'm glad you're happy," Eva said truthfully. It was about the only positive thing she could think to say. Good thing Sienna wasn't here. Eva would grab her by the shoulders, look her straight in the eyes and yell, "Are you freakin' kidding me?"

"Ryan is the greatest guy in the world." For the next ten minutes, she rhapsodized about her fiancé's stellar qualities. According to Sienna, Gandhi paled in comparison.

Bitter much? The voice at the back of Eva's mind needled.

"Tell me you're going to finish nursing school first," Eva said.

"Oh, yes, absolutely. The wedding is scheduled for next June right after graduation."

"What does Angie think?"

"Oh, you know Mom, she's cool about everything.

It's Dad who's a tiny bit upset that I'm getting married so young."

Of course Angie was cool with it. Eva swallowed. She was acutely aware of how different her childhood had been from her younger sisters'. When Eva was growing up her mother had insisted she call her by her first name so men wouldn't think she was old enough to have a daughter Eva's age. Sienna and their younger sister, Brenna, got to call her Mom like normal people.

Until Angie had married Sienna's dad, Mike Shoemaker, Eva's life had been chaotic. They'd never lived in one place for long as her mother traipsed from town to town, guy to guy, trying to "find" herself. And while Eva was grateful that Angie had finally latched on to a decent guy like Mike, she and her stepfather had never really bonded.

It was clear enough that he considered Eva Angie's daughter, while Sienna and Brenna were his. He had honestly tried to connect with her, but they'd just never found common ground beyond Angie. If Eva were being honest, she'd admit most of it was her fault. She'd just kept waiting for Mike to take off on them like the others had and by the time she realized that he wasn't going anywhere she'd been all grown-up.

The hollowness in her stomach deepened, but Eva shrugged it off. She wasn't the type to wallow in the past, wishing that circumstances had been different. She was pretty good at making the best of things, but along with that hollowness was just a tinge of jealousy. It wasn't fair that Sienna who was nine years younger had already found her soul mate.

Come on, you don't even believe in that soul mate malarkey.

"So," Sienna said, "I'm hoping you'll be my maid of honor."

"Of course," Eva agreed.

In spite of the stiff relationship she had with her stepfather, she loved her younger sisters with a fierceness that surprised her. She couldn't be jealous of Sienna's happiness even though part of her wished she, too, could know what it was like to fall head over heels in love with a guy worth giving up her freedom for.

Since when? She'd never even really thought about marriage—which might explain why she kept hooking up with guys like Keith.

But now, she was twenty-nine. Twenty-nine with no birthday cake, no presents, no card, not even a damned phone call.

This is what happens when you're footloose and fancy-free.

"Eva," Sienna said, "I'm so, so happy. I want you to be this happy some day. How are things with Keith?"

"We broke up."

"Oh, I'm so sorry. And here I was going on about how wonderful my life is."

"No need to be sorry, it's no big deal. Keith certainly wasn't my soul mate."

"Do you think that um…maybe…" Sienna paused.

"What?"

"Well, that maybe the reason you can't find a keeper is because you rush into relationships? I mean Keith is like what? Your fifth boyfriend in two years?"

Guilty as charged. She did tend to rush into physical intimacy. A flush of embarrassment, combined with irritation, burned her neck.

"Sixth," she admitted.

"I didn't mean to make you mad. I shouldn't have said anything."

"No, no, feel free to speak your mind."

"It's just that I want to see you as happy as Ryan and I are, Eva. So next time you meet Mr. Maybe why not take things a little slower?"

Yeah, I'll get right on that. "Uh-huh."

"Don't worry. You're going to find someone," Sienna said in a perky, cheerleader voice. "Love will get you when you least expect it."

Twenty years old and she was talking as if she knew everything. Eva pressed three fingers against her brow and massaged away her irritation. "I'm really happy for you. And don't worry about me. Now go celebrate."

"Thanks." Sienna paused. "I love you so much."

"I love you, too," Eva said.

"Bye."

"Good night." She hung up and stared into the darkness, waiting, feeling as if she was caught in suspended animation. It scared her. This weird sensation of not belonging anywhere, never fitting in.

"To hell with self-pity," she muttered, threw back the covers, stripped off her pajamas and headed back to the living room. She wasn't going to let getting dumped and turning twenty-nine and playing maid of honor to her kid sister get her down.

Three minutes later, the candles were lit, Enya was crooning lyrically from the iPod and Eva was deep into Triangle Pose while the soft ocean breeze ruffled the curtains in front of the open window.

And as she exercised, all her embarrassment and irritation vanished and in its place she felt a strange sense of peace, as if someone out there was watching over her.

3

Eva loved summer in Southern California. Warm but breezy. Not too hot, not too cold. Blue skies, bright sun. Not many clouds to speak of. On rare occasions you might get a thunderstorm, but it usually happened only once or twice a year.

Two days after her conversation with Sienna, Eva lay listening to the soothing music whispering through the ear buds of her iPod as she floated on the inflatable raft in the apartment complex pool. The air smelled of chlorine and hibiscus blossoms. Colorful umbrellas spread out over poolside patio tables. They were all empty. Everyone was at work.

She smiled. God, she loved her job that allowed her to be home when most people were working. Monday through Friday she gave classes in the early mornings and then again in the evenings, but the middle of the day belonged to her. Saturday was her busiest day, when she ran back-to-back classes from 6:00 a.m. to 1:00 p.m. Of course, since she owned the studio, she popped in from time to time to make sure everything was running smoothly, but she hired good people. There weren't many problems.

For all her mother's traipsing from town to town, state to state, Eva had learned one thing. She was a water baby, through and through. Being around water made her happy. It didn't matter if it was ocean or lake, river or pond, or even just a swimming pool, whenever she was near water, she felt balanced.

Her best friend Zoey told her it was because she had Aquarius rising in her horoscope. Eva didn't even know what that meant, but she did know that surf, sun and sand made her feel extraordinarily alive and she loved living in San Diego.

She closed her eyes behind her shades, felt the wind skim the fine hairs around her navel. Ah, peace and quiet.

Then an odd prickling sensation tugged at her stomach. Someone was watching her. She could feel it.

Eva opened her eyes.

A man stood poolside staring down at her, a white trash bag in his hand. He was well over six feet tall with broad, ruler-straight shoulders and solid biceps bulging at the seams of his navy blue T-shirt. He wore white shorts that hit just above tanned knees, and running shoes. He looked both comfortable in his own skin and utterly in charge of the space around him.

For a second or two, she thought that he was a mirage, conjured up by her sun-softened brain. Then she realized that nope, this hunk was the real deal.

She was suddenly aware of how she must look to him, lounging on the float in her bright red bikini, her blond hair tumbling about her shoulders, her body slick with perspiration. She took a deep breath, envisioned pulling her navel to her spine as she taught her students in yoga class, and then tugged the earbuds from her ears, pushed her sunglasses up on her forehead and met his gaze.

"Like what you see?" she drawled impishly.

His steady gaze heated her up like a hot lick. "Sorry," he said, not looking the least bit apologetic. "I didn't mean to stare…"

"And yet here you are, still staring."

Was it her imagination or were the tops of his ears turning red? But he did not look away. Embarrassed and bold. An unexpected combination that gave him a charming vulnerability.

"I just moved in and I was wondering where the Dumpster was located." His deep voice seemed to blow the words across her skin like a child's breath at a dandelion bloom.

Why did she have a feeling that taking out the trash was simply a ruse to come down and say hello to her? She felt flattered, but immediately squelched the emotion. No more jumping willy-nilly into superficial relationships with good-looking men. She was twenty-nine now. She had to start thinking about the future.

She cleared her throat. His intelligent dark brown eyes swung back up to sharpen on her face. He came across as calculated, measured, self-assured. His equanimity both unnerved her and piqued her curiosity.

"The Dumpster is that way." She pointed toward the back of the complex. "Just beyond the laundry room."

"Thanks," he said, but he didn't move. He just kept standing there.

Eva felt self-conscious and wished her cover-up wasn't spread across a lounge chair on the opposite side of the pool.

He dropped the garbage bag, and she watched it fall because she simply couldn't continue holding his intense gaze.

Watch it. Remember you're turning over a new leaf.

No more skimming the surface when it comes to relationships. From now on, it's either all or nothing.

"Name's Adam," he said, "Adam Mancuso."

Then with his hand outstretched, he moved toward the edge of the pool, the material of his shorts molding against his muscular thighs.

He leaned down. She reached up.

Their hands touched.

Sizzle.

There was no other word to describe the slam dunk of his forceful sexuality ramming into hers. She'd had many boyfriends in her life. Shaken hands with many a good-looking man, too, but she'd never felt anything quite like this jolt of instant attraction.

Involuntarily, she licked her lips. "Eva. Eva St. George."

His hand lingered on hers. His gaze pinned her to him like a corsage to a lapel, but he said nothing.

"So, Adam," she said desperate to fill the silence before she said something totally inappropriate like *my place or yours?* "What brings you to San Diego?"

"How do you know I'm not from San Diego?" He dropped her hand and straightened, but didn't back off.

She shrugged, peered up at him, kept her belly sucked in. "You've got that East Coast vibe."

"East Coast vibe, huh? What does that mean?"

"I don't know, you seem..." She paused. "Formal."

An eyebrow shot up on his forehead. "You can tell all that about me in five minutes?"

"My mom moved around a lot when I was a kid. I've lived in thirty-three states."

"Really? I..." He seemed like he was about to say

something else, but then he just stopped, as if monitoring himself. "That's interesting."

"That's East Coast, too."

"What is?"

"Holding back until you get to know someone."

"Maybe my holding back has nothing to do with the fact that I'm from the East Coast. Maybe it's just my personality and I would be just as withholding if I'd grown up in Southern Cal."

"Could be," she agreed. "It's probably something of a stereotype, anyway, that West Coast people are initially a lot friendlier, but you never get to see behind their masks whereas East Coast folks might be more standoffish at first, but once they accept you, you're like family."

"You've given this a lot of thought."

"I suppose I have," she mused.

"What about Southerners?"

"They'll kill you with kindness. Watch out when they bless your little heart."

"And Texans?"

"They're a whole breed apart," she said, and then grinned. "I was born there."

"Ah, so you chose to become a California girl."

"What can I say? I love the fair weather."

He hummed a line from a Beach Boys' song about California girls. That was unexpected, too. He didn't seem the kind of guy to spontaneously burst into song. Intrigued, her gaze strayed to the ring finger of his left hand.

Bare.

She struggled not to grin. A bare ring finger didn't mean anything. He could still be married or in a committed relationship. He could be a flirtatious playboy after as many notches on his bedpost as he could collect. But that wasn't the read she was getting on him. Then again she wasn't exactly a great judge of character— Keith a case in point. Eva jumped too easily into relationships and she knew it. Even her baby sister knew it. She'd taken after Angie in that respect.

"You're starting to get a little pink." He waved at her shoulder. "Just above your collarbone."

"Oh." She touched her shoulder. It did feel a bit hot and achy. "I must have missed a spot with the sunblock."

The bottle of sunscreen lay on the chaise with her cover-up. He went for it. "Float on over here and I'll rub you down."

Suggestive words if she'd ever heard them, but he delivered them with such a straight face she couldn't decide if he was playing coy or not.

Did she dare?

Before she could make up her mind, he snagged one end of her float with the toe of his sneaker and trolled her toward him.

His eyes met her. They were an amazing shade of earthy-brown—the color of autumn, a season that didn't exist in San Diego. It made her think of warm wooly sweaters and football games and fall festivals and bonfires all hot and crackly.

Her stomach fluttered.

Stop it.

"Here we are." His low, deep tone feathered over her ears, raised the hairs on the nape of her neck. He was so close.

Too close.

Intimate.

She breathed faster, anticipating his touch. The

bottle of sunscreen made a soft whooshing noise as he squeezed out a ribbon of milky white lotion and the aroma of fresh coconut scented the air.

"Lean forward," he instructed.

Compelled, she leaned forward, positioning her shoulder closer to him, and pulled her hair back off her neck. Why was she obeying him? She was annoyed with herself but she just kept sitting there with her torso cocked forward, giving him access to her back.

His hand slipped over her shoulder, the cool balm soothing her heated skin. His breath caressed the top of her ear. Her muscles tensed at his touch.

"How's that?" he murmured, massaging in the cream.

"Mmm." She meant to say, "Mmm, that's enough." But after the *mmm,* the rest of the words stuck in her throat and the *mmm* just hung there sounding all sexy and encouraging when she hadn't meant it that way at all.

His broad fingers spread out over her shoulder. The watch at his wrist ticked softly. He smelled crisp and clean, like fresh cucumbers and spray starch. Her float bobbled on the water.

The whole thing felt like some weird, languid dream. Had she fallen asleep on the float and conjured him up in her slumbering mind? Why else was she allowing a stranger to stroke sunscreen across her shoulders?

Annoyed with herself, she put a hand on the cement lip of the pool and pushed away from the edge. "Thanks," she said, feeling breathless and out of sorts. "You saved me from a sunburn."

"Happy to help." He straightened and wiped his palms together, massaging the remaining lotion into his hands.

She chanced a glance at him. He looked as rattled

as she felt and she had a sneaking suspicion he wasn't the kind of guy who normally went around offering to lather up strange women. So why her? Why now?

"Well…" he said.

"Well," she echoed.

He leaned down, picked up the trash bag. "See you around."

"Yeah, see ya."

He walked away and Eva let out the breath she hadn't even been aware she'd been holding. Adam. Hmm. Adam and Eva. She couldn't pair up with this guy if she wanted to. Their names were just too cutesy together.

Pair up? Are you nuts? Here you go again, closing your eyes and jumping into quicksand with both feet. Snap out of it.

Snap. She was snapping out of it. No more fantasies about…

Adam walked past her again on his way back from the Dumpster. Her thoughts trailed off and she cocked her head to get a better look at his backside. Hard, defined, the perfect size. Yum!

He strode with military bearing, straight-backed, stiff-legged and confident. His stride proclaimed that he was accustomed to being in charge. She sensed something more. He was alert, intelligent, the kind of reserved yet responsible man that a woman could trust. A shiver passed through her. Was he Navy? She had a few Navy guys take her yoga classes. They usually showed up because someone had told them they had trouble letting down their guard and relaxing and had suggested yoga.

"Hey," she called out.

He stopped, turned in her direction. "Yes?"

"If you ever want to loosen up, I teach yoga at a studio just down the street. First class is free."

"Loosen up?"

Why had she said that? Why was she inviting him to her yoga class? What in the hell was she thinking? Adam and Eva.

Oh, God, stop it.

He stalked back toward her, his brown eyes murky and unreadable and at the same time incredibly magnetic. "Do I look like I need to loosen up?"

"Um…no, no," she lied as goose bumps spread over her body. Goose bumps. The guy was giving her goose bumps.

Remember Keith? He was good-looking and made you go all goose-bumpy the first time you saw him. That didn't last long.

"I'm just trying to drum up business," she said.

A spark of amusement flared in his eyes as he gazed down at her. "Who knows? Maybe I'll just take you up on your offer and come learn Downward-Facing Dog."

Then he walked off leaving her with the delightful image of Adam Mancuso with his scrumptious butt in the air.

Eva lowered her lashes. Hmm. With him moving in next door and her determination to lay off casual affairs, it was shaping up to be one very long hot summer.

ADAM TOOK THE STEPS UP TO his apartment two at a time, his thoughts centered squarely on the woman in the pool.

An intriguing woman who—from the minute he'd seen her doing naked yoga—had intrigued him in a way no woman ever had. But it wasn't just her kick-butt body that aroused him. It was something about the combination of her easy-breezy attitude and her sharp intelligent blue eyes that turned him inside out. Eva St. George was a woman of substance and that unexpected realization made him want to know more. How had such a smart woman gotten mixed up with Barksdale?

He shouldn't have engaged her in conversation and he knew Rogers was going to bust his balls about it. He'd used taking out the trash as a ruse to get a closer look. He hadn't meant to say anything to her, much less rub her shoulders.

And dammit, he'd stared straight at her tits like a caveman. They'd perched ripe as summer peaches in the sling of her bikini top and her smooth, flat stomach... well, *hell!*

Her long legs had been bent at the knees, drawn up slightly on the float. He'd been trained to observe everything so he didn't miss the pearly pink nail polish on her toes or the gold ankle bracelet or the double diamond studs gracing her earlobes. Her golden-blond hair floating around pink shoulders in need of sunscreen...

Ah, those shoulders. His palms still tingled from touching her and he could smell her coconut-scented sunscreen on his skin.

Face it. She'd entranced him. Eyes the color of the Pacific Ocean. Lush, feminine thighs built for loving.

Tanned skin and full, glossy lips that he somehow knew would taste like plump California strawberries.

He shouldn't have been lusting after her. It was wrong. It put his job in jeopardy. It worried Adam that he hadn't been able to stop himself. He'd flirted with her, taken advantage of the situation, used potential sunburn as an excuse to touch her.

"What the hell was that all about?" Rogers launched

in the minute the door closed behind Adam. "We're not supposed to engage the target. Merely observe and report."

"We've been doing that for four days and we've gotten nothing," Adam hedged, scrambling to think of a good reason why he'd stopped to talk to Eva.

Rogers stared at him as if he'd sprouted a third eye in the middle of his forehead. "Since when have you not followed the rules to the letter?"

Adam frowned. "I want Barksdale caught, and sitting here on our hands doesn't seem to be doing the trick. If I get to know her, maybe I can get her to talk about Barksdale and I can find out something NCIS didn't when they interrogated her."

"Hey, I agree with you. I've just never known you to take matters into your own hands. Why do you think they call you Kiss Ass Mancuso?"

"Who calls me that?" Adam asked sharply.

"Everyone." Rogers wrinkled his nose. "You didn't know?"

Irritation had him shoving his palm over his head. "Just because I believe in obeying orders doesn't mean I'm a kiss ass."

"You're a workaholic."

"Yeah? What's wrong with that?"

"You never let your guard down with the guys. Even the few times you have gone out for drinks with us, you barely drink and you leave as soon as you can."

"I am a naval intelligence officer. We're held to a higher code. I don't intend giving my enemies anything they can use against me."

"That doesn't mean you can't relax once in a while, chief. Act like one of the guys."

That had been Kirsten's complaint, as well. That he

was too compulsive about work and didn't know how to enjoy himself. Were Kirsten and Rogers right? Honestly, having free time on his hands made him anxious. The truth was, he feared that if he ever dropped his vigilance that the floodgates would open and he'd lose all control.

"That's why I think it's kinda cool that you're ready to bend a few rules in order to nail Barksdale."

Adam hadn't said that. In fact, he hadn't meant to bend rules. It had happened because he'd simply been unable to help himself and that scared the shit out of him. Eva St. George scared the shit out of him. He wanted to have sex with her and the promise of that pleasure lured him and that lure made him feel unbalanced. He'd given into temptation.

"You know," Rogers said, "if you wanted to hang out at her yoga studio in the evenings, I could keep watch on the apartment while you're gone. You could cozy up to her. See if you could get her to talk about Barksdale."

Adam shook his head. "The brass wouldn't approve."

Rogers sank his hands on his hips. "How would they know?"

"They've got Kilgore taking yoga with Barksdale's suspected contact."

"That's a morning class. You can take an evening class."

It was tempting. Not just the part about catching Barksdale himself, but about spending time with Eva.

Watch it, you're on shaky ground.

Temptation could ruin a man. He trusted Rogers as much as he trusted anyone, but Adam had a hard time putting his fate in someone else's hands.

"Nah," he said. "Let's play this by the book."

Rogers shrugged. "Your call."

Adam glanced out the window and saw Eva climbing from the pool, her body glistening in the sunlight. His own body reacted. His dick hardened and his heart rate quickened. He was in trouble and he knew it. He'd never felt this out of control. One thing was for certain he was *not* going to her yoga studio.

No matter how much he might want to.

4

IT WAS 5:30 A.M. THE FOLLOWING morning and Adam's shift was almost over. He yawned, stretched, dreamed of hitting the shower, and then getting some sleep as soon as Rogers woke up to relieve him. He wasn't really paying much attention to what was going on across the courtyard. Eva had been quiet. No midnight yoga. No striptease in front of the window. All in all a pretty boring night.

He yawned again. Blinked.

The door to Eva's apartment opened and she stepped out onto the landing, wearing a thin terry cloth bathrobe that hit her midthigh. The pockets of the robe bulged out.

Hmm, where was she going in her bathrobe at five-thirty in the morning? And what did she have in her pockets? Immediately, he perked up and his mind went to the darkest possibility. Was she packing a gun?

Come on, how likely was that?

Still, he was on red alert, adrenaline humming through his bloodstream.

It wasn't just her looks or her smoking-hot body that stirred him. The attraction he felt for her—and this was worrisome—extended far beyond the physical. She was funny and witty and spirited. All the things he was not and he admired her for it. The woman was high-energy, high-octane, high-stakes and these oddly respectful feelings he felt for her presented a problem.

She started down the stairs. Adam tracked her with the telescope, watched her cross the courtyard and head toward the walkway leading to his side of the complex. She disappeared from his view. What was she up to? He tensed, got up from the stool.

Footsteps sounded on his staircase.

She was coming to his apartment!

Panic seized him and he wondered why in the hell he was panicking.

Because she was coming to see him!

He couldn't let her get a peek inside. Not with all the surveillance equipment aimed at her apartment.

Shit! He pulled a hand down his face. What was he going to do? He could pretend he wasn't here but it was five-thirty in the morning and the Nissan Maxima Higgins had given him to use while he was on assignment was in his parking space and—

Her knock sounded at his door.

Maybe he ought to answer it. What if she was in trouble? What if Barksdale had threatened her?

She knocked again.

Adam rushed to the door, but only opened it a crack. He peered out at her with one eye. "Hey."

"I'm sorry to wake you up—"

"I wasn't asleep." He opened the door just wide enough to slip out onto the landing with her.

Dew dampened the air. The sun nudged at the horizon. The complex lay quiet. Normally, he got up at 5:00 a.m. to go for his daily three-mile jog, but ever since he'd been spying on Eva, everything in his world had turned topsy-turvy.

She stared at his rumpled clothes, his beard stubble, and then glanced at the door. "Oh, my gosh, you've got an overnight visitor. I'm so sorry. I shouldn't have bothered you. Go back to your guest."

Eva turned to scurry away, but Adam reached out to snag her arm. The minute he touched her, he regretted it. Hot desire instantly flooded his system. "Hang on, what's wrong?"

"It's nothing, really," she said. "I don't want to take you away from your company."

"Who says I have company?"

"You didn't invite me in for one thing." She cast a roving glance over him. "And you look like you've been up all night."

"I don't have a woman in my apartment."

"Oh, okay, if that's the way you want to play it."

"Why? Are you jealous?"

Her cheeks pinkened, telling him that yeah, she was and she wished she wasn't. He felt flattered.

"No, of course not. I'm not jealous. Why would I be jealous? I don't even know you."

"And yet here you are on my landing at five-thirty in the morning in your bathrobe." Okay, he was officially acting like an arrogant ass, but it was only because she smelled so good and she was wearing a bathrobe and his surveillance equipment was only a door away and she was jealous and well, hell, she just made him nervous and he really didn't know what to say to her so he said something utterly stupid.

"Forget it." She held up both palms, backed off.

"That was a jerky thing to say."

"It was."

"I'm not usually a jerk."

"I'll reserve judgment until I know you better."

"Does that mean you'll give me a second chance?"

"Only because you're so cute when you grovel. Apology accepted."

He wouldn't call it groveling, but he did need to find out why she'd come over. "Seriously, what can I do for you?"

Her gaze flicked downward, just for a microsecond, but she checked out his zipper. Had she seen that he was halfway hard already? He did his best to get himself under control, but it was a losing battle with her standing there smelling of fabric softener and peppermint toothpaste, the encroaching dawn casting orange fingers of light over her golden hair.

She cocked her head, touched her bottom lip with the tip of her index finger. "The hot water heater went out in my apartment and I was wondering if I might borrow your shower."

"You want to borrow my shower?"

"That's what I said, but if you have a woman in your apartment—"

"There's no woman in my apartment," he reiterated, even though the smart thing to do, from the point of view of his assignment was, yeah to let her think there was a woman in his apartment so she'd go away.

Except, he didn't want her to go away. He wanted to throw the door wide-open and invite her inside. Of course, he couldn't do that, wouldn't do that but he wanted to.

"How about if I come over and take a look at your hot water heater?"

"I called the super. He'll be over later today to check it out. I just need a quick shower to start the morning. I brought my own supplies." She reached into the pockets of her robe, pulled shampoo from one pocket, conditioner from the other and looked pointedly over his shoulder at his door.

Adam's hands were behind him, holding the knob, blocking her way. "Here's the truth. I'm a pig. The place is a mess."

"How bad can it be? You just moved in."

"I've still got boxes stacked everywhere." He couldn't get the image of her standing naked in his shower out of his head.

"Look, if you don't want me using your shower, just say so."

"It's not that," he said, grasping at straws. "You're right, I have company, but it's not a woman. I have a friend staying with me. We partied. He's passed out drunk."

"So, I'll tiptoe. I really need a shower, Adam."

"I don't…" He fisted his hands. He'd run out of excuses. Short of being rude and telling her to buzz off, he had nothing.

"Oh, I get it." Her eyes widened and a sly grin curled her lips.

"Get what?"

"You don't want your friend seeing me in my bathrobe."

The minute she said it, he knew it was true. He didn't want to risk Rogers waking up and seeing Eva in her bathrobe, dripping wet from her shower. "You got me."

"Hmm," she said.

Hmm? What did that mean?

"You don't have to be jealous."

"I'm not jealous," he lied. "My friend is a caveman."

"Ah, so you're trying to protect me?"

"Chivalry, that's what I'm all about."

"You're an odd duck, Adam Mancuso."

What was he supposed to say to that? "C'mon. Let me take a look at your hot water heater. I bet I can get it up and running."

"You're handy like that?"

He held up both hands. "Guilty as charged."

"I've never known a guy who was very handy."

"Well, now you do." Even though he'd grown up privileged, his parents had insisted he learn as many practical skills as he could to make him a well-rounded person. In high school, he'd taken both building trades and Latin, automotive repair and physics.

She shrugged. "Okay."

"Okay," he echoed.

She stuck the shampoo and conditioner back into the pockets of her robe and turned to head down the stairs. He followed after her, his mind in free fall.

God, but she was amazing. The woman was self-possessed enough to saunter over to the new neighbor's place in her bathrobe and ask to use his shower. She had an easy way about her, like a carefree daisy swaying in the breeze and a mass of gorgeous blond hair and sassy blue eyes that stared into his as if he was a crossword puzzle she couldn't wait to solve.

Was it weird that he found that as compelling as her tight little rump bouncing with each step she took down the stairs?

He followed her over to her apartment, thinking that he would follow that sweet ass straight into hell if that's where she led him. How had he gotten to this point, desire short-circuiting his brain *and* his code of ethics? Troubling.

Once inside her apartment, his military training took over. He scanned her place, taking it in with a cataloging glance.

Minimalistic Scandinavian furniture, numerous candles and an incense burner on the mantle of the gas fireplace, a bookcase loaded with books about exercise and nutrition (physical fitness, something they had in common), a beige jute rug over the flooring and two surfboards. One was a large, colorful old-style surfboard mounted on the wall that seemed to serve as a decorative shelf and the other, propped in the far corner, waxed and gleaming in the dusky sunlight that peeped through the partially open drapes.

The room felt as if it was a temporary skin. Something she'd yet to shed. He didn't know where the impression came from. Maybe it didn't come from Eva or the room at all, but from him. As if he were the one on the verge of something strange and new and waiting, just waiting, for the future to happen.

He shook his head, shook off the feeling. "You surf?" he asked, a topic bland and safe.

"Pretty much every other person in San Diego surfs. We *are* less than two miles from the beach. It's why I live here."

"Big-time hobby, huh?"

"Passion is more like it."

Funny, that passion hadn't made it to her dossier. "I thought yoga was your passion."

She studied him a long moment, her eyes pinning him to the spot. He shifted, uneasy and that unexpected uneasiness rippled under his skin, hot and restless.

"I'm a woman of many passions," she said evenly, but the corner of her eye twitched.

A tic?

Was she hiding something? Or was she slyly winking at him? Flirting?

He wasn't adept at flirtation. It was a custom too light, too playful to suit him. Flirting opened the door to other things. Things he had no business thinking about.

Adam pressed his palms together, closing that door on his thoughts. "Take me to your hot water heater."

"In there." She waved him down the hallway, indicating a closed closet door.

He stepped by her, accidentally grazing her shoulder as he went past. Audibly she sucked in her breath. Was she as aware of the sparking between them as he was? Damn, but her hair smelled like a flower shop and there was that very shapely body that even a shapeless terry cloth robe couldn't disguise. Bewitching.

His cock stiffened.

She's your target. Stop thinking about her as a woman.

Yeah, that was like telling a spawning salmon not to swim upstream. It shocked him—this total lack of control. He hadn't been this horny even as a teen.

He forced his mind off her and on to the hot water heater. He opened the closet door and peered in at the gas appliance.

"Can you fix it?" Eva asked, coming to peer over his shoulder.

Her breath was warm against his skin. She wasn't touching him, but almost. An odd splitting sensation hit him squarely in the middle of his chest as if his very center was cracking wide-open.

"It's just the pilot light," he mumbled. "We'll shut it

down for a few minutes, let the gas disperse and relight it. All will be well." With that reassurance, he closed the fuel line, the closet door and his unruly libido.

EVA PERCHED ON A WHITE wrought iron bistro table underneath a Cinzano umbrella on a wooden deck overlooking the Pacific in La Jolla, mentally riding a wave. She drew in a lungful of air, breathed in the dynamic smell of the ocean and thought of Adam.

He was like the fetching white caps off in the distance, surging and full. But whether the energy between them was going to fade into nothingness or become a navigable wave hinged on a number of factors. Waves could die out or swell depending on wind, tides and bathymetry. The influences were myriad.

Lazily, she fantasized about an A-frame wave. Big and voluminous that formed with distinct shoulders on either side of the crest. A-frames allowed two surfers to enjoy the same wave, one riding frontside, and the other backside. Just thinking about it made her hot. Reaching up, she fingered the puka beads at her throat.

Daydreaming of Adam was dumb. She knew it. So why had she used her broken water heater as an excuse to traipse over to his apartment? She could have showered at her yoga studio, but once she'd seen a light on in his apartment, she'd been over there like a shot. Hadn't she learned anything from Keith? Was she going to go through her life wearing her heart on her sleeve, jumping from man to man just like her mother had until she'd finally found Mike?

Ultimately, what did she want? Was it a husband and kids? Was she simply letting her birthday get to her? Where was all this self-doubt coming from? She'd always been fairly self-assured, why the disequilibrium? Why now?

"Gosh, I'm so sorry I'm late." Her best friend, Zoey, rushed over to the table, shopping bags in her hand. She leaned over to kiss Eva's cheek.

She wore a floppy white straw hat and designer sunglasses. Zoey was a natural redhead who burned instead of tanned. She had on a gauzy white top and matching white slacks and lots of jangly jewelry. She deposited her bags in an empty chair and sank down across from Eva. Beside her, Eva felt frumpy in denim capri pants and a button-down print blouse.

"So how was Spain?"

"Fabulous. I could have stayed another month." Zoey waved her hand. The sunlight caught the extravagant diamond on her left ring finger.

"Zoey!" Eva leaned over and grabbed her friend's hand. "What's this?"

A huge grin split Zoey's face. "Jason popped the question. We're engaged!"

Eva hopped up out of her chair and ran around to embrace her friend in a big hug. "Ooh, I'm so excited for you. Guess what? Sienna just got engaged, as well."

"No kidding. This is so exciting."

"Let's order mimosas to celebrate."

"None for me," Zoey said. "I'll just take some iced tea."

"Oh wow, oh gosh, that's one honking ring." Eva took hold of Zoey's hand and examined the diamond thoroughly.

A snarl of fierce jealousy lashed through Eva so strong that it took her aback. She wasn't the jealous type. Why did she suddenly have a heavy feeling in the pit of her stomach?

A waitress came over and took their orders for raspberry iced tea and fish tacos.

"Don't think I forgot your birthday," Zoey said once the waitress had gone. She pulled a gift-wrapped package from one of her shopping bags.

"You didn't have to get me anything," Eva protested, but secretly she was touched that at least one person had remembered her birthday.

"Of course I did. You're my best friend in the whole world."

Tears misted the corners of her eyes. She wasn't an overly emotional person but for some reason she was feeling sentimental today.

Eva undid the package wrapped in a red ribbon and opened the box. Inside, she found a silver charm bracelet with symbols of Spain—a tiny silver bull, a matador's hat, a flamenco dancer, the Spanish flag and a cluster of olives. Eva slipped the bracelet onto her wrist, admiring it in the sunlight.

"For my footloose and fancy-free friend." Zoey raised her glass of tea in salute. "Long may you roam. Someone has to keep the faith with the single life.

Eva's chest tightened and she felt…*what?* Regret? Wistful? What was wrong with her? Why was she feeling so melancholy? Usually, she was very upbeat. Did it have something to do with her new neighbor? Or could he be the cure for the malaise that unexpectedly ailed her? When had she become known as a nomad?

"Eva?" Zoey asked. "Are you okay?"

"Sure. Fine." Eva forced a smile. "I just feel like… well…how does that song go? About rowdy friends all settling down?"

"For one thing," Zoey said. "Sienna was never rowdy."

Eva smiled. "That's true."

"For another, just because I'm getting married doesn't mean we won't be hanging out together."

Yes, it does. But she didn't say that, of course. She didn't want to rain on Zoey's parade. This was her big news. Eva forced a smile. "Sure we will."

"We'll make a weekly lunch date. Fish tacos in La Jolla."

"To fish tacos and friendship." Eva raised her glass and tried to ignore the sadness seeping through her bones.

Nothing was ever going to be the same again and she knew it. No late night partying on the town until two in the morning with her best friend. Their time together had already been curtailed when Zoey had started dating Jason. It was only a natural progression.

"You know that I'm expecting you to be my maid of honor," Zoey said.

"I wouldn't have it any other way. When are you getting married?"

"September."

Eva set down the taco that she had half way to her mouth. "Zoey, that's only three months away."

"I know." Zoey's cheeks reddened.

"Why so fast? What's the ru—" She broke off as she realized what the rush could be. "You're pregnant?"

Zoey looked hesitant, then nodded. "That's why no mimosa for me."

"Zoe!" Eva was out of her chair again and around the table to envelop her friend in another exuberant hug. "That's wonderful!"

Zoey looked relieved. "Oh, thank God. I was more worried about telling you than I was about telling Jason."

"Really? Why?"

"Because I knew Jason was mad for me and that he'd propose. I knew everything was going to be okay on that score. He's a rock, my dude—kind and steady and hardworking. Not like the losers I dated before him."

Eva had had her share of losers, too. She thought of Keith and then immediately switched gears and thought of Adam. What a world of difference.

There was just something about Adam that called to her, something that sent a little thrill into her stomach. It wasn't just his lean, muscular body and good-looking face that affected her. The determined set to his firm chin told her he wasn't a quitter. Whatever he did—a job, a relationship, a project—he was in it for the long haul. And that was scary to a butterfly like her.

But while his chin could turn flinty with determination, there was a kindness to his eyes not often seen in adamant men. A kindness that spoke of a deep inner calm, a serenity of the soul that she'd never been able to accomplish, not even in her practice of yoga. That serenity called to her. Adam was a man who knew himself. He was certain and sure and she found that confidence very appealing.

Don't be nuts. You don't even know Adam. You've talked to the man exactly twice. Two times does not a first impression make.

And yet, he *had* made an impression on her. One she couldn't shake. Talk about a rock. And in more ways than one. She grinned. He was firm, centered and self-possessed. A man you could count on.

You don't know that. Stop fantasizing about him and focus on Zoey.

"So why were you dreading telling me?" Eva placed a hand over Zoey's lower abdomen.

Zoey touched Eva's hand and their eyes met. "I'm worried about you."

That startled her and she eased her hand away. "Whatever on earth for?" she asked, trying to sound light and breezy, but not sure that she succeeded.

"I don't want her to come between us." Zoey cradled her belly.

Eva's world brightened. "So the baby is a girl?"

"I'm only nine weeks into this, so we don't know it, but I just have this feeling it's a girl."

"Zoey, this is such happy news." Eva hugged her again.

"I thought you might be sad."

"Why would I be sad? This is a baby we're talking about. This is the biggest thing ever."

"There will be no more late nights for us."

"That's okay. Late nights are overrated. Look at the up side. No more walks of shame."

"No more bad date stories."

"No more sitting home alone on a Friday night."

Zoey grinned. "Thank heavens that's over. I feel like my real life has finally begun."

That last statement was a kick in the teeth. Eva knew her friend didn't mean it the way it sounded, but it left Eva feeling as if she were in limbo, waiting to start her "real" life with a husband and a baby. The fact she felt that way bothered her.

She'd never been one of those women who believed she needed a family to feel complete. She'd been independent since she'd left home at seventeen, moving to San Francisco and attending Berkeley for a year before dropping out to travel and try a variety of jobs. School just hadn't been her thing.

It wasn't that she hadn't gotten good grades, because

she had. But she'd possessed an entrepreneurial attitude and a love of physical activity. Starting her own business made more sense to her than hanging out at school for four years. Maybe she'd missed out on a lot. Maybe she was still missing out.

Things were changing and there was nothing she could do to stop it.

She smiled her way through the remainder of the meal, doing her best not to let envy creep in, but when her cell phone rang, she snatched it from her purse, grateful for an excuse to stop talking about weddings and babies.

That is, until she read the caller ID.

Unknown caller.

She never answered unknown calls. They could leave a voice mail and if it was important, she'd return the call. She muted her phone, stuck it back into her purse and turned her attention to Zoey. "So, have you thought of any baby names yet—"

5

EVA COULDN'T SLEEP. SHE LAY in her bed, thinking about Sienna and Zoey getting married. About Zoey having a baby. It wasn't that she wasn't happy for them, because she was. Rather, she couldn't shake the feeling that she was getting left behind. She'd come home from her lunch with Zoey to find a belated birthday card from her mother and somehow that had made her feel even lonelier.

So to keep from thinking about such things, she thought about Adam instead. Which was a huge mistake. A picture of how he would look naked kept popping into her head.

Frustrated, she finally tossed back the covers, stripped off her pajamas and headed to the living room to do yoga. She lit candles. Put on music. Stood in the middle of the floor to do some deep breathing.

Then she stopped and walked to the window, and peeked through the curtains at the apartment across the courtyard. She imagined that Adam was over there, watching her in the darkness.

It was an intriguing fantasy and she found herself nudging the curtain open just a little bit.

She realized suddenly she'd never seen him leave the complex. His car was in his parking spot when she left for work. It was there when she returned. Hmm. Perhaps he worked from home.

Such a shame. A man who looked like that shouldn't be cloistered from the world. He could have been a centerfold. Six-one. Dark hair. Cut too short, but still sexy. Except for the hair, he looked sort of like Daniel Day-Lewis in *Last of the Mohicans*. He had that same air about him. Serious. A warrior. Dedicated to a cause. She found his personality traits incredibly arousing. Hawkeye. She sighed dreamily.

She pretended he was over there on his side of the courtyard, staring at her, arms crossed. His dark eyes hooded with lust. Instantly, her chest tightened and she felt slightly out of breath.

Her breasts ached, her nipples hardened.

She moved to the sofa, still fantasizing that he was watching her. She peeled off her panties, lounged on the cushions and spread her legs, her fingers trailing to where her body was rapidly growing hot and wet. The room smelled of candle wax and her overheated sex. She closed her eyes and an erotic daydream claimed her.

Against the back of her eyelids, she saw Adam.

"Eva," his throaty voice called her in a sultry, velvet-smooth croon that sent shivers rafting through her.

Her pulse quickened as she envisioned Adam in the room with her, taking off his clothes in a slow striptease. Her nipples grew even harder, straining upward for his imaginary mouth.

She could almost feel Adam's broad hands gently stroking her skin, skimming over her breasts, moving lower, circling her navel, teasing her pitilessly.

Whimpering, Eva lightly pinched one of her tender

nipples, pantomiming what she wished Adam would do to her. She sank her teeth into her bottom lip and with her eyes still closed, slowly explored her body.

Ah, yes. This was good. This was what she needed; a little sexual release to end her frustration.

Greedily, she caressed the naked flesh between her thighs and all her pent-up energy slipped out on a sweet sigh of pleasure.

Adam.

How she wanted him to kiss her. Hold her. Stroke her. Sink his hard cock into her. She slid her fingertips over her achy skin, across her silky folds, skimming along the satiny moisture oozing from her swollen inner core.

"Adam," she whispered.

She saw him leaning over her on the couch, his hand fondling the delicate bud of her feminine arousal. She felt his mouth touch her there, burning and bold. Her heart thundered and her mind spun.

Oh yes, oh yes.

In her mind's eye it was his hand dipping between her legs, caressing and rubbing her swollen clit. He kissed small circles against her inner thigh and with his other hand he was doing exotic things to her bottom.

Her fingers moved in time to the fantasy as imagination and reality blurred sweetly. She could feel the orgasm starting deep within her.

Yes, yes.

It gathered, strengthened, built.

She stoked the vision, feeling his large penis pressing against her, tasting his lips on her tongue. The orgasm was almost there. She was so close. Only inches away.

Come.

Faster and faster her fingers strummed and she increased the pressure, in a rush now to achieve her goal. Relief. Release.

"Adam," she whispered, and thrashed her head against the couch pillow. "Adam, Adam."

She imagined being with him, this man she craved. She wanted to look into his eyes while he made love to her. Wanted to stare into the core of him and touch that inner strength that made her feel so welcomed, cared for and cherished.

She was on fire now, burning from the inside out. And there was Adam watching her with ravenous eyes. His desire for her evident, his penis erect. He was pushing aside her fingers, sliding into her, dilating her, taking her.

The orgasm hit, ripping through her like a lightning storm. Gale force and exhilarating.

Her legs stiffened. Her back arched. Eva cried out and shuddered as satisfaction lit up her body.

She came hard.

But in the end, it wasn't nearly adequate enough. She lay on the couch panting for more. Her orgasm, no matter how good, was steeped in loneliness. She felt as if she was in a vortex, sucked empty. Dry.

No matter how sweet the fantasy, it couldn't make up for what she lacked.

She wanted Adam. Needed him. Here. His body buried deep inside hers.

ACROSS THE COURTYARD, Adam stood watching and he could not believe what he was seeing. Eva engaged in self-pleasure.

Was this a wet dream? Was he asleep fantasizing that he was spying on her as she lay on her couch stroking herself? If he was, this was the best wet dream ever.

Eva St. George was the most amazing woman and he had ringside seating to her peep show. Not only was she sexy as all get out, but her spunky chutzpah aroused him, as well. He respected how she went boldly after what she needed. He liked how she threw herself into experiences the way he threw himself into his work. She showed him how to be spontaneous and flexible. He admired how easily she shrugged off setbacks and didn't let problems get her down. Her free spirit magnetized him. She set him on fire.

He should walk away, he knew that, but he also knew that he wasn't going to. He fisted his hands, swallowed hard, and blinked against the sweat suddenly running down his brow.

Her body glowed in the candlelight, slick with perspiration. He watched her lightly pinch her nipple with one hand while the other hand moved down, down, down.

He'd never seen a more arousing sight. Her long fingers, the short nails painted with a clear gloss, tracking over her bare skin, headed for the place he most wanted to be. His breath came in hard, quick pants. His dick was cement. His balls ached painfully.

His fingers went to his zipper. All right. He was going to do it. He was going to pleasure himself. But just for relief. Just to keep himself from slamming out the door, stalking over to her apartment and taking her right there on her sofa.

He palmed himself, curled his fingers around the head of his cock. He imagined her soft moans. Blood shot straight to his groin. He swelled, grew.

Her fingers moved rhythmically, her juices glistening. He could see the sweet little hood of her sex, jutting up pert and hungry.

He held his breath, his eye glued to the eyepiece,

unable to tear his gaze away from the stunningly erotic sight. She was so moist and pink and beautiful down there.

Her fingers grew more frantic. Her back arched and she thrashed her head against the soft cushions.

His own hand was busy; matching her stroke for stroke, imagining it was her hot little fingers on his cock. Pressure gathered in his balls, pushed upward. He could feel it building in his shaft. Release was imminent.

Her soft sounds of pleasure were driving him insane.

He moved the telescope slightly so he could zero in on her face. Her teeth sank into her bottom lip, a furrow creased her brow and she looked as close as he was.

Faster and faster Adam stroked himself.

And just before he came, he saw Eva's body jerk and he swore he saw her call out his name.

THE VERY NEXT EVENING, Eva was mildly surprised (and a lot delighted) to look out at her 6:00 p.m. hatha yoga class and see Adam lurking at the back of the room with a yoga mat tucked underneath his arm. She hadn't really expected him to ever show up, but she was glad he was here.

She'd been thinking of him a lot lately, especially after what she'd done in her living room last night. Her thoughts of him had been compounded when she'd listened to her voice mail and heard Keith's voice begging her to call him back.

When hippopotamuses fly.

She was done with Keith. He'd caused her to be questioned by NCIS. If nothing else had come from the relationship, she'd gotten very clear on what she did not want. She'd even momentarily considered changing her cell phone number, but it seemed more hassle than it was worth. He'd only called her the one time in the three weeks since she'd seen him last. He'd get the hint when she didn't call him back. Keith had his faults, but he'd been pretty astute.

Adam wore cargo shorts that in spite of their bagginess managed to show off his tanned muscular legs. Not the best yoga attire, but she suspected there'd be no way to get this man into Lycra. Not that she even wanted to try. He was far too masculine for that. In fact, he almost seemed too masculine for yoga, but she loved that he was giving the practice a chance.

Maybe he's not here for yoga. Maybe he's just here to see you.

Her stomach fluttered at the thought.

Adam had flirted with her at the pool. He'd made an excuse to touch her. He'd eagerly volunteered to come check her pilot light. He stopped to speak to her every time they passed in the courtyard.

Their eyes met across the room crowded with students and she felt the sweet pierce of his gaze.

It bothered her, this attraction. Mainly because she knew Sienna was right. That she too easily followed her compulsions. Like last night, when she'd done what she'd done on the couch with the curtains partially open, imagining Adam was watching her.

What if he *had* been watching her?

A thrill fluttered through her at the possibility. Eva dropped her gaze, went over to the controls for the sound system and turned on soft, relaxing music with the undertones of waves crashing.

In her mind's eye, she could see the beach, smell the surf, feel the grit of white sand beneath her toes and hear the palm trees swaying in the wind. Impulsively, she wished she were on the beach with Adam, totally alone and naked.

Eva gulped, struggling to get herself under control.

Something had given way in her last night. Broken loose. Something as unfathomable and surprising as a riptide. She turned to face the class again.

"Deep breath everyone," she called. She drew in a deep breath, pulling her navel to her spine, demonstrating the technique.

The class complied.

"Inhale," she coached. "Hold it." As the sound of the surf rolled out, she said, "Exhale. That's right. Feel your body relaxing with each breath. Inhale…exhale."

After a couple of minutes of deep breathing, the students were looser, all except, she noticed, for Adam. He stood stiff as a soldier on patrol.

And so was she.

Her muscles tensed. Her throat constricted. She'd unconsciously mirrored his posture. This wasn't good, an uptight yoga instructor.

Concentrate. Focus.

She loved her work. Loved yoga. Loved the calm energy the practice brought into her life. It was the perfect antidote to her hopscotch thoughts, stabilizing both her body and her mind. When it came to yoga, usually nothing threw her off her game.

Adam Mancuso appeared to be an exception to the rule.

"Mountain Pose," she called out, demonstrating the basic standing pose designed to bring the body into alignment. Right now, her own body and thoughts needed serious realignment.

"Now Salutation to the Sun. Feel the stretch. That's

it." She cast a glance at her students. Everyone was doing well.

Except for Adam. He was off balance, teetering.

"Let your feet and calves root to the floor. Imagine you are an old oak tree, immovable, strong."

Adam wobbled, his forehead creased in a frown.

"Now just breathe." She paused.

Adam finally stabilized, and looked pleased with his accomplishment.

She ducked her head to hide a smile. "Okay, very good. On your mats now for Butterfly Pose."

She got down on the floor to demonstrate the pose, sitting up straight and bringing the soles of her feet together in front of her. "Wrap your fingers around your toes and gently pull your heels in toward your groin."

The students followed her lead, Adam included.

"Keeping your back straight, slowly lean forward from the waist as far as you can. Don't force it. You should feel a good stretch in your pelvis. Great. Long, slow, deep breaths."

Soon the room filled with the sound of controlled, rhythmic breathing. It was bizarre—she'd never really noticed before *how* erotic yoga could sound.

"This pose is also used in Kundalini yoga," she reminded the class. Repetition was a teacher's stock in trade. You repeated and repeated and repeated until finally, drip by drip, your students caught on. "The Butterfly Pose not only promotes flexibility, it also raises your sexual energy center. Don't be alarmed if you have some unexpected physical reactions to this practice. Your bed partners will be delighted."

A woman in the back row sitting beside Adam tittered and Eva had to resist rolling her eyes. Some people could be so immature about sex. It was just a bodily function. No different from any other.

"Let's shift to Cow Pose and inhale."

The class moved as one with Adam being the lone exception. He stayed in Butterfly Pose.

"Exhale into Cat Pose."

They complied, but not Adam. What was the deal? Was the guy hung up on butterflies?

Eva got to her feet and moved among the students, stopping to correct postures as she went. She continued to call out instructions to the class as she got closer to Adam.

He was still in lotus position while the other students were down on all fours. Was he afraid of putting himself in a vulnerable position? She'd had male students who were and refused to do certain poses.

Eva reached the back of the room and leaned over to murmur, "Is there a problem?"

He looked sheepish. "Um…sort of."

She glanced downward. He had his hand draped over his lap and he looked extremely self-conscious.

Immediately, she understood what must have happened. Sometimes, when men performed the Butterfly Pose they got a spontaneous erection. Usually, it only happened to experienced yogis whose sacral chakras were highly sensitized. When it happened to a novice, it was an indication that he had a lot of natural prowess and with the proper training could be aroused to great tantric heights.

Eva decided not to share this with him. It was too much personal information in a nonintimate setting.

"It's nothing to be ashamed of," she said.

"You might think this is no big deal," he whispered

tersely, a fierce frown on his face. "But it's damned embarrassing. I feel out of control."

"You have to let go of control in order to experience your real strength."

"What the hell does that mean? It doesn't even make sense."

"It makes perfect sense when you think about it. Until you let go of the need to control, you can never be fully *in* control."

"Well, it feels very inappropriate to me. I can't…it won't…go down."

Eva became aware that the class had stopped their Cow-Cat Pose rotation and had turned to see what was going on at the back of the room.

"Pose of a Child," she commanded.

In unison, the students obeyed, going face-down, arms extended, knees tucked to their chests.

"Wow," Adam said. "Crack that whip."

"Give me your hand."

"What?"

"Give me your hand," she repeated.

"What for?" He tilted his head up at her, but kept his hands protectively sheltering his lap.

"Do you want help with your problem or not?"

"I don't think you get how this works. The touch of a gorgeous woman is *not* going to alleviate things if you get my drift."

"It will."

"It won't."

She extended her palm. "Hand," she insisted.

Adam looked as if she'd suggested he stick his finger into a live electrical socket.

"Gimme."

Reluctantly, he shifted his arm to block her view of his groin and stuck out his left hand.

THE SECOND EVA TOUCHED him, the boner that had arisen when he'd struck the Butterfly Pose got even stiffer, just as Adam had known it would.

For the first time in his life, he was having uncontrollable erections and it was all because of her. Even when he'd been a hormonal teen, he'd been able to douse unwanted sexual stirrings by focusing his mind on somber thoughts. But not now. Not after watching Eva do naked yoga, among other things, through the narrow opening in her living room window.

He was a voyeur. A spy. Watching in the darkness.

It wasn't the yoga that had caused this graphic response. Rather, it had been the sight of Eva's lithe body stretching into easy contortions, her intoxicating rump in the air. The image of how she'd looked on the sofa last night was forever branded in his brain.

He'd tried not to think about her. To focus on his breathing and all that other Kundalini stuff. But hell, she'd been sitting up there in front of him, her legs spread in butterfly position and he'd been aching for her for days.

Why had he come here? He knew he shouldn't have come here. He'd told himself he wasn't going to come here. But he had not been able to make himself stay away. She'd called his name in the middle of the night as she'd given herself an orgasm. He hadn't hallucinated it. And now that he'd come here, his dick was also desperate to come.

Eva's nimble fingers traced over his hand and then she pressed her thumb squarely in the middle of his palm and rubbed.

Hard.

Who knew the center of your palm was so damned sensitive to pressure? It felt as if every ache in his body had suddenly converged there, responsive and raw.

"Is it going away?" she murmured.

"No."

She kneaded harder.

"That's not helping."

"Relax."

"Seriously?"

"Hey," one of the students called out. "How long are we going to stay in this pose?"

"Cobra Pose," she called over her shoulder. Then to Adam, she whispered, "Just breathe."

When she said it, he realized he'd been holding his breath. Who knew breathing was such a tricky thing?

She ran her thumb along his palm just below his fingers and massaged each joint individually. It wasn't the least bit sexual, but his boner wasn't going anywhere. He could smell her rich scent—part perspiration, part cherry scented shampoo. He could feel the heat of her body.

"Does that help any?"

"No," he croaked.

"Pull your spine upward."

That he could do. Years of military training had given him excellent posture. He straightened his back, felt some fringe of self-control return.

And then she reached down and placed her palm against his diaphragm.

Her hand.

On his belly.

Inches from his dick.

"Inhale from the bottom of your heart," she instructed.

What the hell did that mean? He closed his eyes, tried to imagine his heart breathing.

A hot flush raced through him. In a flash, he saw stars, felt silk sheets, tasted the sweetness of her lips and felt the heat of their bodies joined in sex.

His eyes flew open. Her face was only inches from his. Her hand still on his belly as she bent over him, her bottom lip caught between her teeth.

God, but she was incredible and he didn't know what was more disturbing—her sudden gesture of vulnerability or the fact that his erection had suddenly vanished.

"Are you—"

"I'm fine," he gruffly cut her off.

When her gaze dropped to his lap, Adam did something that surprised them both. He reached up and touched her lips.

When those gorgeous ocean-blue eyes met his, he felt it again, except ten times stronger—a mind-bending jolt of pure sexual awareness.

And bam! The boner was back.

Dammit.

"Oh, dear," Eva exclaimed.

"Yo, teach, what's up?" hollered a male student. "This cobra can only go so long without striking."

Eva sprang away from Adam and hurried back to her place at the front of the room. "Downward-Facing Dog."

Butts went in the air.

Adam took advantage of the position shift. He scrambled to his feet, yanked his yoga mat off the floor and, holding it in front of him to camouflage his condition, made a beeline for the door.

6

RELIEF SAGGED THROUGH EVA at Adam's departure.

Not because she didn't like him, but because of how much she did. It was too soon after Keith to get involved with someone. Especially a man she knew absolutely nothing about. A man who compelled her in a way no one had ever compelled her. That was the real issue. Compulsion. It couldn't be healthy.

You're imagining things. Romanticizing him. Leaping too fast. He's no more fascinating than the other men you've been with.

Even so, Adam had thrown her off her game, but with diligent focus she made it through the rest of the class.

The way she saw it, she had two choices. She could do what she'd always done. When she saw a man she wanted, she simply went after him without weighing whether he was really someone she wanted to be with long-term or not.

Traditionally, she went for the looks, the chemistry, the sex appeal, which Adam had by the bucket loads. Or, she could ignore the rush of attraction, the thrust of hormones, the heady desire to kiss him until her lips swelled. She could be sensible for once when it came to relationships and follow her head instead of her ovaries.

She thought of Sienna who seemed very happy getting married to the only guy she'd ever dated.

Then she thought of her mother. How Angie had gone from one handsome guy to another, jumping into relationships without looking, taking Eva along with her. The roller coaster of her mother's multiple relationships hadn't ended until she'd gone for the safety and security of Mike's kindness over good looks and a bad boy temperament. Then she thought of tempestuous Zoey who seemed very ecstatic over laid-back Jason and their baby on the way.

Eva had one thing going for her—she wasn't dragging children through her mess of a love life—but she was making the same mistakes her mother had made. Assuming lust meant love. Well, it was time to stop that nonsense. She was twenty-nine years old.

Twenty-nine.

The innocence of youth was gone and what did she have to show for it besides a butterfly tattoo on her shoulder?

No. It was time to get off the merry-go-round and start acting like an adult. She was not going to allow this attraction to Adam Mancuso to turn her head.

Absolutely not.

ADAM EMERGED FROM THE ice-cold shower he'd taken in the locker room just as Eva's yoga students emerged from her classroom.

It was rotten timing for his emotions—his gut constricted the minute he laid eyes on her and he had an overpowering urge to turn and run—but it was perfect timing for his assignment. They could walk home together and he could strike up a conversation, see if he could get her to talk about Barksdale. Besides, he wasn't a coward. When he was afraid of something, he faced it head-on.

"Hey," Eva said, a hesitant smile flitting about her lips. "You okay?"

He felt the tension in his own smile as he lied. "Fine." *Only after the cold shower cure.*

"You were headed home?"

"Yeah."

"Did you drive?"

"Walked."

"Me, too. Would you like to walk home together?" she asked, beating him to the punch.

"Um…"

"I only ask because I thought you might want to talk about what happened in class. Yoga can produce some startling reactions in our bodies and it's only natural to be alarmed."

Adam suspected his physical reactions had nothing to do with yoga and everything to do with the pert, fresh-faced yoga instructor. Even simply standing here in the hallway, staring into those big blue eyes, he could feel his dick rousing again. He tightened his jaw, determined not to let testosterone get the better of him. He really didn't want to talk about what had happened, but it was the perfect excuse to engage her in conversation.

"Yes," he said. "I'd like that very much."

"Great. Just let me get my bag."

He stepped out of the way of the door and waited while she zipped into the locker room and then returned with an oversized tote bag slung over her shoulder, her purple yoga mat peeking from the top.

The summer night air was warm, but not overly so. People strolled the sidewalks. They passed a Thai restaurant spilling the smell of ginger, peanut and coconut out into the street.

"That's a great place to eat," Eva observed.

"Is it a good place to take a date?"

"The atmosphere isn't terribly romantic," she conceded, "but the food makes up for it."

"I'll keep that in mind."

"Do you have a girlfriend?"

"Not yet," he said, not knowing why he gave that answer.

She cast an appraising glance over him. "How long has it been since you've been in a relationship?"

"Um…"

"Okay, that was too nosy. It's none of my business."

"A while," he admitted.

That was true enough. He and Kirsten had been broken up for almost a year and he hadn't been with a woman since. Honestly, that was probably what was wrong with him. A year without sex could do serious damage to a guy's restraint.

"That could explain your intense reaction in class," she said. "That and the fact that you have a really fiery sacral chakra."

"Fiery sacral chakra?"

"It means you're just naturally very sexually responsive."

That comment made him inordinately proud of himself. "I'm not sure I believe in all that chakra business."

"You don't have to believe it. Doesn't change the fact you're chock-full of sexual mojo."

"I am?"

She made a noise in the back of her throat that almost sounded like a purr. "You have one of the strongest masculine auras I've ever seen and I've seen a lot of them."

"You read auras, too?"

She shrugged. "My mom worked in a spa in Sedona for a couple of years when I was a kid. I guess I absorbed some of that culture."

"It's a different philosophy," he said, not wanting to sound judgmental, but he found all the New Age stuff a bit far-fetched.

"Yeah," she said. "You have to be pretty open-minded to believe in it."

Oh, so he wasn't open-minded? "There's open-minded and then there's gullible."

The soft smile was back at the corner of her lips. "Are you saying I'm gullible?"

"No, it's just that there's two sides to every argument."

She nodded, surprising him by agreeing. "My mom's the gullible type, but my childhood experiences didn't turn me off to possibilities. There's plenty of mysteries in the universe."

"Are you saying I'm turned off to possibilities?"

"Not at all, but you seem to be taking it that way. Why is that?" She canted her head.

Eva had the ability to make him doubt himself and for a man who was always certain of the path he was on, that was unsettling. They crossed the street at the stoplight.

From this spot on the hill he caught a glimpse of the ocean stretching below. It was a beautiful place to live. The town houses they passed all had window boxes growing a plethora of colorful flowers. He had the strangest urge to pick a handful of blooms for her.

"I'm saying not to cut yourself off to possibilities, Adam. You seem to have already made your mind up about the world."

"What makes you think I'm doing that?"

She stopped walking and he had to back up. Her gaze fixed on his face. He shifted under her scrutiny.

The woman was sharp, looking as if she could read his every thought. It was disconcerting, her talent for sizing up a situation. She made him feel…well, not so alone…and that put him on guard instantly. She was charming and disarming and he wanted to move mountains for her. More cause for concern.

"What are you so afraid of?" she asked.

You. "Who says I'm afraid of anything?"

"Everyone is afraid of something."

This conversation was spiraling out of control and he didn't know how to rein it back in. "I'm afraid of getting an erection in yoga class."

Her laugh was clear and loud and the sound of it stirred something joyous inside him. This woman did strange and wondrous things to him and *that* was what scared him more than anything else.

"Touché," she said. "I take it you won't be returning to class."

"I didn't say that."

Her eyes lit up. He could tell that she liked him. He liked her, too. That was the issue.

"So," he said, "you know I don't have a girlfriend. What about you?"

"I don't have a girlfriend, either," she teased.

Delightful. She was delightful. He had to watch this one. She kept him on his toes. "No man in your life?"

Slowly, she shook her head. "No, but I'm not looking for a relationship."

"Did the last one burn you pretty badly?"

"How do you know there was a last one?"

"Beautiful, sexy woman like you? I'm betting there have been a lot of guys chasing you."

She shrugged. Not coy, admitting it. "The last one burned me, but not in the way you think. He didn't break my heart or anything. I wasn't that invested. More like he hurt my pride. Since then I've been thinking about a moratorium on dating."

"For how long?"

"A year."

"Why's that?"

"I tend to jump into relationships too fast and end up with the wrong kind of guy, so I'm thinking maybe I should take a year off and get to know myself a little better. I fear I might be one of those women who always has to be with a man, and that's not how I want to be."

"What makes you say that?"

"Well, I've never really been without a boyfriend since I was sixteen. Boyfriend. That sounds like such an immature term when you're pushing thirty."

"You're almost thirty?"

"Just turned twenty-nine."

"I would have guessed you weren't more than twenty-five." This was true even though the dossier the ONI had compiled listed her date of birth.

"You don't have to flatter me. I'm not sleeping with you."

Her honesty took him by surprise. He was accustomed to game playing from most women. "I don't recall asking you to."

Her gaze traveled below his belt. "Your penis did."

The way she said "penis" only made him more flustered. "Hey, I thought you said it was a natural reaction to that particular yoga position."

"You're not doing a yoga pose now."

Adam gritted his teeth. The woman was outrageous.

"You embarrass so easily," she said. "I think it's adorable."

"I'm not embarrassed."

"Then why are your ears red?"

It was all he could do not to finger his ear. Instead, he was stunned to hear what came out of his mouth next. "My ears turn red when I get turned on."

"Oh," she said. "Oh."

Ha! At last she was at a loss for words.

Awkwardness stole over them and the night air was suddenly filled with a heavy undercurrent of tension.

"How come a woman like you isn't already married?" he asked, desperate to say anything to fill the void.

Eva smiled. "What do you mean, a woman like me?"

"Sexy," he said. "Smart. Inventive."

"I have many flaws."

"Yeah? Like what?"

"I'm dreadfully honest and drink orange juice straight from the carton."

"Those *are* terrible flaws," he murmured. "But you'd think some guy would have braved them for the total package."

"I could ask you the same thing. Are there any serious relationships in Adam Mancuso's past?"

"There was one," he admitted.

"What happened?"

"We were too much alike. Kirsten realized it before

I did and called the wedding off. She said she needed a man who completed her, not complemented her."

"Sounds like she'd already met someone else to me."

"You're intuitive, as well, Eva St. George."

"Not as much as I should be," she said.

"What does that mean?"

"I've had several misguided relationships. If I was more intuitive, I never would have gotten involved with some of those guys in the first place."

"Oh?" He leaned closer. "Do you want to talk about it?"

She wrinkled her nose. "Most guys don't want to hear about a woman's exes."

"I don't." He fisted his hand. "But if it helps you to talk about it…"

"Not really. What's past is past…" She lapsed off.

"What was his name?"

"Keith Barksdale."

Ah, they were getting somewhere at last. Adam waited, not wanting to seem too curious.

She swallowed, moistening her lips with her tongue. "It was…he was…"

"Yeah?" Adam said, fisting his hand. "What'd he do?"

"He was charming. Very good-looking." She glanced down, then raised her eyes and met Adam's gaze. "But not as good-looking as you."

"No?"

"You want to get some ice cream?" she asked, stopping in front of an ice cream shop.

"I don't normally eat ice cream."

"You don't like it?"

"I love it, that's the problem." He patted his belly.

"One cone," she said. "What could it hurt?"

It wasn't the one cone that bothered him. It was the thought of her wicked little tongue licking at the smooth, creamy confection. He was about to beg off, but she was already opening the door of the shop, pushing inside. "C'mon."

Without really knowing why, he went.

"A scoop of pistachio on a waffle cone," she told the girl behind the counter. "And..." Eva turned back to Adam, but didn't wait for him to order. "Vanilla in a cup."

Was he that damned predictable that she could so easily guess his ice cream preference?

"Put mine in a waffle cone, as well," he said just to be contradictory.

"Ooh." Eva's eyes twinkled. "Mr. Plain Vanilla likes a bit of crunch with his cream."

"How did you know vanilla was my favorite?"

She held up both palms. "I'm intuitive."

"Impressively so. More lessons from Sedona?"

"Not really. Vanilla *is* the number one flavor. I took a wild guess. The odds were in my favor."

Sassy. He liked that.

They got their ice cream and meandered past a family of six sitting at the front of the store, bickering good-naturedly.

"You ever think of having kids?" she asked when they were back on the street.

"What?" That question seemed to come out of left field.

She inclined her head toward the family inside the ice cream shop. "You'd be great at it."

The comment pleased him. He did want a family.

Eventually. Someday. Maybe. "What makes you say that?"

"You strike me as the responsible type."

"Is that a compliment or a criticism?"

"Depends on if you want to be responsible or not."

"Do you want kids?"

"Someday, I suppose. My best friend, Zoey, just found out she's pregnant. Luckily, her boyfriend is a great guy and he proposed. They're getting married in a couple of months."

"I suppose that's one way to do it."

"How would you do it?"

"I'm a pretty traditional guy. I'm a fan of the marriage first, baby second option."

"That option doesn't guarantee happily ever after."

"Maybe not, but it's the way I feel."

"Me, too. At least for me. Other methods work for other people."

Her agreement surprised him. He would have supposed she'd be unconventional about parenthood. "You're pretty balanced, Eva St. George, you know that?"

"All those years of yoga," she joked.

"Why yoga?" he asked, pausing to take a lick of his ice cream. "What's the appeal?"

"I'm attracted to the discipline."

"Oh?"

"Yeah, growing up I didn't have much of it."

"That nomad thing you were talking about."

She nodded. "My mother had wanderlust and a kid. It's not the best combination in the world. What about you?"

"My family moved around a lot, too."

"What's the story there?"

"Military."

"Ah, that explains a lot."

"It does?"

"Explains why you're so self-possessed. Most military brats I've known vanquish their social neurosis at a young age, if they ever had one. I think it's more than just moving around. I mean my mom moved around but I never felt comfortable in one place for very long. Not until San Diego. Military people seem to have the ability to just pick up and go and make the best of whatever situation they land in. It always took me forever to settle in and make friends and then, poof..." She snapped her fingers. "Angie would be up and gone again."

"Angie?"

"My mom. She's only eighteen years older than I am and she likes for me to call her Angie."

"She sounds like an interesting person."

Eva tossed the remainder of her ice cream cone in a nearby trash bin. "She used to be pretty avant-garde. Now, she's a normal mom."

"Why the change?"

"My stepfather. He's the anchor to her bobbing sailboat. They're good for each other. He keeps her grounded, she keeps him from being such a stick-in-the-mud."

Eva stopped walking. They'd arrived at their apartment complex. He could just leave things as they were, say good-night and hightail it to his apartment. Or he could gallantly offer to walk her to her door, as he would have under any other circumstances.

"Well," she said. "That was entertaining."

"C'mon, I'll walk you to your door."

"I'm perfectly okay to climb the steps on my own."

"I know you are. I just want to make sure you get home safely."

"You live just across the courtyard."

He took her elbow and for a moment he thought she was going to jerk away from him, but instead, he felt her relax into his grip.

"Okay," she said. "Fine. If you get your jollies over being a gentleman, I'm not opposed to being walked to my front door."

"Good." He guided her up the cement walkway lined with long stem red flowers that swayed in the breeze.

Their sneakers made muted sounds that echoed softly throughout the courtyard. A few people were in the pool, laughing and talking, but no one was near the staircase leading up to Eva's apartment. They reached her door. She inserted her key, opened the door, and then stepped over the threshold. She turned around, paused.

Adam had an irresistible urge to kiss her, but he would not. He had to draw the line somewhere. He had to—

Before he could even finish the thought, Eva leaned over and planted a quick kiss on his cheek. "Good night, Adam Mancuso, you odd man, you." Then she shut the door.

A hundred different feelings, none of which he could rationalize or fully identify, rushed over him. Chagrin, longing, desire, foolishness, disappointment, relief.

He turned and hurried down the stairs. Strangely, it seemed wings were attached to his shoes and he didn't even register the journey from her door to his. Her lip print was branded on his cheek, his skin tingling from where she'd touched him. He hadn't been this befuddled since high school. What the hell was going on? He was a Navy officer in the ONI. He wasn't some nerdy geek infatuated with the prom queen. He had to get control of himself. This had to stop.

Fully expecting to be taunted and teased by Rogers—he knew his coworker had been watching Eva's place—he turned his key in the lock, his mind already spinning excuses for his behavior, only to pull up short at what he saw in the living area.

It wasn't Tim Rogers seated on the stool beside the telescope; it was his boss, Commander Higgins.

7

AFTER SHE CLOSED THE DOOR behind Adam, Eva floated into the kitchen. She kicked off her shoes and opened the refrigerator door, then took out a bottle of orange juice, twisted off the top and took a long drink. Her lips still throbbed from where she'd kissed Adam's cheek, it had been faintly shadowed with beard stubble.

Why had she kissed him? Resisting the man was difficult enough. She was playing with fire, asking for trouble and yet she couldn't seem to help herself.

Eva put the cap back on the orange juice, and headed for the shower. She tried not to think about Adam, but she could still smell him on her skin, masculine and clean. She could still feel the grip of his hand around her elbow, strong and protective.

She gulped. She was moving too fast, reading too much into the dangerous pull between them. Having naughty sexual fantasies about him.

Calm down. Take a deep breath. Stabilize yourself. You don't even know this man.

Okay, all right. Snap out of it. She was snapping out of it.

She shed her clothes, dropping them in a trail as she

made her way to the bathroom. She wondered what had motivated him to come to yoga class. Was he interested in her? Or was he serious about yoga? Maybe it was both. He did say he'd moved out here to make a fresh start. Try new things in his life. Maybe she was one of those new things.

You don't have to be one of his new things. Just because you're both interested doesn't mean it has to lead anywhere. You could just be friends.

What a novel concept. She'd never been just friends with a guy. She wasn't sure how to go about it.

She took a shower and then went to the living room to pick up her clothes and stuff them into the laundry basket. She made herself a snack of Wasa crackers and low-fat cheese and perched on the couch to watch television. Her eyes kept straying to the open window.

From her peripheral vision, she could see the window of Adam's apartment. What was he doing? Was he thinking of her as she was thinking of him?

Why was she thinking of him? Sure, he was good-looking with a body to die for, but come on. A lot of guys were good-looking with killer abs.

What was it about *this* guy that seemed to have so wholly captured her imagination? She knew nothing about him, but maybe that was part of the appeal. Once she learned more about him, she'd probably grow bored. That's how it usually happened for her. When a guy no longer held her interest, she dropped him.

Except for Keith, who'd dropped her before she'd had a chance to drop him. It was the first time that had ever happened.

Then again, he'd done her a favor. She'd been honestly able to say that they'd broken up when NCIS had shown up at her studio flashing their badges.

Remembering, Eva gulped. She'd dodged a bullet with Keith.

She was in the bathroom toweling her hair dry, when she heard her cell phone ringing. She padded to the bedroom where she'd left it on her bureau. Leaning over, wet hair slapping the back of her neck, she took a peek at the caller ID.

Unknown Caller flashed on the screen and she didn't recognize the phone number, so she didn't pick up. She waited a minute and then checked for voice mail. The automated recording told her she had one new message.

She punched Play but all she heard was a moment of male breathing, followed by a click as he hung up.

"COM-COMMANDER HIGGINS," Adam stammered, immediately snapping to attention. "What are you doing here?"

This was it. He was about to receive disciplinarian action for going against his orders and making contact with Eva. He'd never blatantly disobeyed orders before and he didn't know why he'd done it this time.

Eva was a wild compulsion he couldn't seem to control. If he were smart, he'd ask to be taken off the case. Clearly, when it came to Eva St. George, he could not be trusted.

Commander Higgins got to his feet, his expression stern but unreadable. The man possessed caterpillar eyebrows that rested low on his forehead. "Sit down, Mancuso."

Adam sat, keeping his back tall and erect, his chin jutted forward, prepared to take whatever punishment was coming his way. "Sir, yes, sir."

"At ease, Lieutenant," Higgins said.

"Yes, sir."

"I mean it, Mancuso, relax. You're too uptight."

Adam took a deep breath and remembered the yoga breathing Eva had taught him. To his surprise he felt the tension in his shoulders dissipate. Maybe there was something to this yoga stuff.

Commander Higgins paced the small area in front of where Adam was seated, his hands clasped behind his back. "It's come to my attention that you've decided to make contact with the target."

"Yes, sir." He hated hearing Eva referred to as "the target," even though that's what she was. The term was dehumanizing, which was the point, but now that he'd gotten to know her, he couldn't put her in that box any longer. Yet another reason he should ask to be taken off the case. He was losing his objectivity.

"There's been a change of plans."

Adam swallowed. Higgins wasn't lowering the boom on him.

Yet.

Higgins had a reputation for taking his time meting out punishment. He seemed to enjoy torturing his subordinates. Although for the most part, Adam stayed on Higgins's good side. Until the whole Barksdale fiasco, that is. He'd been in charge of the project, so he'd shouldered the blame with a stiff upper lip. And he did feel guilty. Somehow he felt as if he should have prevented the theft.

"Rogers has been reassigned."

"He's off the case?"

"No, he's with Kilgore."

"Doing what?"

"They're in Iowa. Barksdale's grandmother has been murdered."

Fear took a sprint up his vertebra. He forced his voice to stay flat, emotionless. "What?"

"They thought at first it was natural causes. She's been languishing in a nursing home for years. But upon closer examination it was discovered the old lady had been smothered with a pillow."

"I thought we had a team watching Granny."

Higgins winced. "That assignment seemed a dead-end, so I pulled our guys out."

Adam said nothing. He knew Higgins was kicking himself over the decision.

"Kilgore and Rogers will be available for backup if you need them. For now, they're putting the squeeze on the contact. We're almost certain he's the one who hired Barksdale to steal the documents. We'll get him soon. In the meantime. I want all your attention focused on Eva St. George."

"It is, sir." That was the understatement of the year. All he could think about was Eva.

"You weren't at your post this evening." Higgins indicated the telescope with a nod of his head.

"No, sir," Adam admitted.

"You made direct contact with the target even though you'd been expressly ordered not to do so."

"I did." No point lying about it. He was caught and prepared for the imminent dressing-down.

The commander nodded. "Good."

He must have heard wrong. "Good?"

"I approve."

"Sir?"

"Sometimes orders are just a suggestion."

"Sir?" he repeated, wondering if he needed a hearing aid.

"When you're on a stakeout you have to play things

by ear. I know that's not the military's bottom line, but I've been in the field. I understand how fluid things can get. I think it's wise that you decided to make the acquaintance of Miss St. George."

"You do?" He couldn't believe it. Not only was he not in trouble but Commander Higgins was praising him for taking matters into his own hands.

"I admire your initiative, Mancuso. You're growing as an officer. I didn't think you had it in you."

"What? To disobey orders?"

"Frankly, yes."

"It goes against my training."

"And yet, you were able to make a judgment call."

"I don't fully understand, sir."

"If I had listened to my gut instead of budgetary pressures from above, I wouldn't have pulled the team off Barksdale's grandmother. She died because I didn't make the right call. So now I'm developing a new strategy because I don't want the same thing happening to Miss St. George."

"You think her life is in danger?"

Higgins nodded his head. "It's possible. Here's my theory. The buyer approached Barksdale—who is considered one of the best computer hackers in the world, which is why we hired him—to steal the prototype for the JK92. They also picked Barksdale because he'd racked up an overwhelming gambling debt and he was vulnerable."

"Or who knows?" Adam said. "Maybe Barksdale used taking yoga at Eva St. George's studio as a way to get to the contact and he offered to steal the plans for the JK92 in exchange for enough money to pay off his gambling debts so he didn't end up in the Pacific wearing cement shoes."

"That's very possible. Yes. So, he manages to steal the plans—"

"Right out from under my nose."

"Don't beat yourself up about that, Mancuso. Barksdale is a genius when it comes to computer hacking and you followed every protocol. You're not to blame for what happened."

Adam clenched his fists at his sides. Even if Higgins did let him off the hook, he couldn't exonerate himself. There must have been some way he could have been more diligent.

"But because you picked up on it so quickly, Barksdale barely had time to get off the base before we were on to him. I'm certain he downloaded the data to a microchip for his own protection. If he'd sent the file directly via computer, he had no insurance that they would pay him and they wouldn't pay him without knowing he had the real deal." Higgins shook his head. "No honor among thieves."

"And he probably used a microchip as opposed to just downloading it to a flash drive because it's much easier to hide."

"Exactly. When we arrested him we went over his person with a fine-tooth comb and we tore his apartment apart. Nothing. We had to let him go." Higgins sounded bitter. "He could have hidden it anywhere, but if he'd put it somewhere easily accessible and he'd already made the switch—info for money—the buyer wouldn't still be in the country."

"Following that line of thinking, he hid it somewhere he now can't get at it because we've got the noose tied too tightly around his neck."

"Exactly." Higgins snapped his fingers.

"You think he hid it at Eva's place?"

Higgins met his stare. "I believe so. But unfortunately, I can't convince a judge to give me a warrant without more evidence that Barksdale involved Miss St. George. He won't even give me a wiretap for her phone."

"You want me to get close to her so I can search her apartment?"

"Not just that, you'd be protecting her, as well. Someone did kill Barksdale's grandmother. Whether it was Miss St. George's student and his cohorts who were putting pressure on Barksdale to fork over that microchip, or the goons who Barksdale owes serious money to, is up in the air. Either way, your girl could be in serious danger. Barksdale is desperate. He's got to make a move and soon."

"Just to be clear," Adam said, anxious to make certain there was no misunderstanding here. "My new orders are to befriend Miss St. George, discover whatever I can about her intimate relationship with Barksdale while at the same time looking around her place for the microchip and acting as her bodyguard?"

"That is correct. Are you up for the challenge?"

He thought about how little control he had over himself around Eva. If he wanted out of this assignment, now was the time to voice his doubts.

Yeah, and never redeem yourself?

"Yes, sir," Adam affirmed. "I can handle it."

8

THE NEXT MORNING, AS HE SAT spying on Eva's apartment, Adam saw her clamber down the stairs wearing a blue string bikini top with denim shorts and carrying a surfboard. He'd been trying to think of a subtle way to get close to her and the surfboard gave him the perfect excuse. He hurried toward the door, hoping to catch her before she left the courtyard.

"Eva!" he called out from the landing.

She stopped, turned, set down the surfboard and pushed her sunglasses up on her forehead. She wriggled her fingers. "Good morning, Adam."

"You going surfing?" *God, what an idiotic thing to say.* She was wearing a bikini and carrying a surfboard. Where else would she be going? For a ride on the space shuttle?

"Yes," Eva said, politely ignoring his stupid question.

He rushed down the stairs, his eyes drinking her in. The woman was gorgeous. Long, tan legs, toenails painted cherry-red today. It made him want to buy whipped cream and snack on her. Her hair was caught up in a high ponytail.

"Hey," he said.

She smiled. "Hey."

They stared at each other for a moment.

"Listen," he said. "Last night I got your message loud and clear, you're not interested in dating."

"Nothing personal." She raked a lingering gaze over his body and her pink tongue flicked out to moisten her upper lip. "It's not you per se. In fact, another time, another place, another life…"

"You've got this moratorium on dating."

"Right."

"I understand and respect that."

"Thank you."

"But you're the only person I know in San Diego."

"You've only been here a week. You'll meet other people."

He inclined his head toward her surfboard. "I've always wanted to surf."

"They have surfing lessons at the beach."

"I know, but I was hoping you could give me a few pointers."

She looked as though she was about to say no, but then she let out her breath through straight pearly white teeth. Teeth he'd love to run his tongue over.

"You'll need a wet suit."

"Okay, could we go buy one?"

She laughed. There was that soft sound again that uncoiled something dangerous inside him. "You want surfing lessons today?"

"You *are* going to the beach."

"You're serious about this? You really want to surf? It's not just an excuse to hit on me?"

"Just surfing, nothing else." He held up a palm as if he was taking an oath. "I promise."

She canted her head and studied him for a long moment and he just knew she was going to say no and he'd be back at square one. But she surprised him. "Follow me."

He followed her out to the parking lot where she tossed her surfboard into the back of a canary-yellow Jeep. Bright and cheery, just like its owner. She seemed supremely confident, swinging up into the driver's seat of the doorless Jeep.

Feeling a bit out of his element, Adam got in beside her and fished around for the seat belt.

Eva started up the engine before he was strapped in and that made him anxious. He wasn't a rule breaker in spite of the fact he'd pushed the envelope on this assignment. As a military brat he'd cut his teeth on protocol and knew what was expected of him. They were out on the street and he still wasn't buckled in.

"What's wrong?" Eva asked, her ponytail bouncing as she bobbed her head.

"What do you mean?"

"You're scowling like you just got bawled out by your boss."

"Sorry," he said.

"No worries. You can scowl at this gorgeous day if you want to. It's your prerogative."

"I don't want to scowl," he said, finally snapping his seat belt into place and his mood immediately buoyed.

"Yes, you do."

"No, I don't, you just smile an inordinate amount. You're like sunshine, smiling all the time."

"Sunshine doesn't smile."

"But it's sunny. You're sunny."

"You scowl a lot, don't you?"

"No," he denied.

"Liar. You've got a little furrow right there." She reached over and planted the pad of her thumb between his eyebrows.

The sizzle of her touch alarmed him. And so did the fact that she weaved onto the shoulder a bit.

"Hey! Watch the road, woman," he growled. Maybe he was a chauvinist, but he liked being behind the wheel of a vehicle. It bothered him to leave the driving to her. That control thing again.

"Why? Did it move?"

"Huh?"

"It's earthquake country. Sometimes the roads will move on you."

"You're joking."

"Sense of humor not your strong suit, huh?" She winked.

"You're an odd woman, you know that?"

"Why, thank you." She straightened, looking like a perky cocker spaniel that had just won best in show at Westminster.

"It wasn't a compliment."

"Oh, so you like a proper woman who doesn't drive a Jeep without doors?"

"I never said that."

"How about some tunes? Let's have music." She reached for the radio dial. A lively hip-hop beat pummeled the air.

Adam made a face.

"What? Not a fan of Snoop Dogg?"

"Not my style."

She eyed him. "Classic music buff?"

"Jazz."

"Really? Like who? Miles Davis?"

"Yeah. You listen to jazz?"

"I listen to everything. Hip-hop, classic, rock and roll, country and western, Celtic. It's all good."

"Never met anyone who likes all kinds of music."

"Well, now you have. Music is the icing on the cake that is life."

"It is one of life's simple pleasures. Something I don't get to enjoy much."

"How come?"

"Too busy working."

"So what do you do for a living?" Eva pulled to a stop at a red light, pushed her sunglasses down on her nose and peered over the rim at him.

"Um…" He was so busy noticing how good her firm supple arm looked as her hand griped the gearshift beside his knee that he almost forgot the cover story Commander Higgins had invented for him. "Accounting."

She pushed her glasses back up. "You're a CPA?"

"Yeah." It wasn't a sexy job and he expected the light to go out of her eyes.

"Oh, that's great," she enthused.

"It is?"

"Maybe you could help me with my bookkeeping. I love being my own boss, except for all the paperwork. In high school I was terrible in math."

"Why don't you just hire a bookkeeper? They're cheaper."

She blew out her breath and her bangs ruffled from the burst of air. "I had one for a while, but she embezzled from me. That added to my trust issues."

"You?" He shook his head. She seemed so easy breezy. "You have trust issues?"

She rolled her eyes. "Out the wazoo."

Her colorful language intrigued him. He wasn't

accustomed to women who talked this way. "Why's that?"

She waved a hand. "Unstable childhood. But I'm not blaming my mother. I'm grown. My issues are my problem, not hers. Although our parents shape us, ultimately, we're responsible for who we become."

He liked her attitude. She took responsibility for her own behavior.

"Oh, dear." She frowned.

"What is it?" He scanned the area, instantly on alert, trying to see what had alarmed her.

"I'm out of gas."

"You don't keep your tank half-full at all times?"

She swung her head around to stare at him as if he was an alien being. "You do?"

"Yes. Not only does it help with gas mileage but—"

The Jeep sputtered, then died.

"Ah, crap." Eva coasted the stalled vehicle to the side of the road. Traffic whizzed by them. "And there you have it. Another one of my terrible flaws. I forget to put gas in the tank."

"You really meant you were *out of gas,* out of gas."

"That's what *out of gas* means."

"Most people say they're out of gas when they're on a quarter of a tank."

"Would those be the same people who keep their tank half-full at all times?"

"It would."

"Too bad you're not with one of those people." Eva unbuckled her seat belt and hopped from the Jeep. "C'mon."

"Where are we going?"

"To push, there's a gas station on the corner."

He got out and followed her to the back of the Jeep. "You get back inside and guide the Jeep. I'll push."

"Don't be silly, I'll help you push."

"Who's going to guide the Jeep?"

"The same person who would guide it if you weren't here."

"If I wasn't here some guy would stop and help you."

She flashed a grin. "I know."

"Get in the vehicle, Eva," he said in his most authoritarian voice.

"Ooh, bossy. Do women usually go for that?"

He pointed at the driver's side. "In."

Her saucy little tongue darted out to touch her upper lip. The morning sun cast a bright glow off her soft skin.

Adam gulped, feeling the chemistry churn inside him. Dammit, he wanted to kiss her. A real kiss this time, none of that cheek smooching bullshit.

Eva turned and went back to the Jeep. He angled his head, watched her magnificent rump walk away. Then he leaned down, putting his shoulder against the back of the Jeep. "You got it in neutral?"

"I do."

"Here we go." Adam pushed and the Jeep rolled forward.

A few minutes later, they were at the gas station filling up the tank. Eva bounced into the convenience store and came back with two granola bars and two power drinks. She tossed one of each to him.

"Stamina," she said. "You're going to need it for surfing."

"Thanks."

"Thank you."

"What for?"

"Not ragging on me too much for running out of gas. I know it bugged you."

"What's the point of nagging you?"

"Exactly. My last boyfriend—" She broke off and shrugged. "But you don't want to hear about that."

Adam tensed. Was she talking about Barksdale? "I don't mind if you need to get it off your chest."

"No guy likes to hear about a woman's ex."

"We're not dating, remember." He needed to encourage her to talk about Barksdale, get as much info as he could, even though he really *didn't* want to hear the details of her relationship with that hose bag.

"No," she agreed.

"We're friends, right?"

"That's still up in the air."

"The trust issues again?"

She wrinkled her nose. "I must be more trusting than I thought to have even shared that with you. It looks like I'm making progress. My therapist would be proud."

"You have a therapist?"

"Is that a bad thing?"

"You don't strike me as someone who needs a therapist."

"She gives me perspective."

"You're something of a paradox."

"What do you mean?"

"Well, you say you have trust issues, but you breezily take a stranger with you to the beach."

"It's a public place and you're not that strange," she teased.

"Then you run out of gas. Most distrustful people would keep their tanks—"

"I know, I know, half-full at all times."

The gas pump made a clicking noise, indicating that the fueling was finished. She holstered the nozzle and screwed on the gas cap. Adam found himself watching her again, admiring the way she moved.

"I'm an extrovert by nature and I really like people. I trust people initially, on the surface, but when it comes to deep down, intimacy…" She shook her head. "I guess I've been burned one time too many."

"The sticky-fingered bookkeeper and that ex-boyfriend you were talking about?"

"Among other things."

"So really, it's not that you have trouble trusting, but that you trust too easily and then get hurt because the threshold of your guard is so low."

She snapped her fingers. "That's it exactly. You're pretty insightful."

Assessing people was part of his training but he couldn't tell her that. She took the receipt that the gas pump spit out.

They were on their way again, traveling the short distance to the beach.

"You never did tell me about the last boyfriend," he prompted.

"You sure you want to hear this?"

"I've got broad shoulders."

She checked out his shoulders, and smiled. "You do."

"Unburden yourself."

Eva hesitated and then said, "Keith was difficult to please. Nothing I did was ever good enough."

"Was that why you dumped him?"

"I didn't dump him. He dumped me."

"What kind of bozo would dump you?" He heard the

disbelief in his own voice. "Seriously, if you were my woman…"

"I'm not your woman," she said. "I'm not anyone's woman. I'm my own woman."

"I know you are. I phrased that poorly. I—"

"Don't worry about it. You care too much about what people think of you."

"What makes you say that?"

She shrugged. "Is it true?"

"Yes," he admitted.

"You don't have to worry about impressing me."

"Why's that?"

"I'm already impressed." She parked the Jeep in a beachside parking area. "C'mon, let's surf."

9

Eva felt decidedly off-kilter around Adam. She was attracted to him and at the same time leery. He seemed too perfect. He made her feel safe and comfortable and that was *not* a good thing. She'd learned you couldn't really trust people, no matter how much you might want to. He'd been right. Her issue wasn't the inability to trust, but trusting too much and then getting hurt because of it. Right now, she wanted to trust him with all her secrets. Not a smart impulse.

Tossing her head, she took her surfboard, zippered in a carrying case, from the back of the Jeep and tried to squelch the sick feeling building in her stomach. Too much. Too nice. The way he made her feel.

"Let me carry that for you."

"I'm perfectly capable of carrying my own surfboard." She swung away from him.

"It looks heavy."

"I've been surfing for ten years. I've developed the muscles for it."

"I feel like a lame ass letting you do the heavy lifting."

"Down, Sir Galahad. You're in California now. Girls

carry their own surfboards all the time. Besides, you'll soon have your own to carry."

He said nothing, but she could tell from the expression in his eyes he still didn't like it. This one had a chivalrous streak she found far too appealing. In the past, she had depended too much on men, no doubt a legacy from her mother. But when that tendency had gotten her into some complicated relationships with men who tried to tell her what to do, she'd shrugged off that dependency and taken control of her life.

She liked what she had going now, running her own business teaching yoga. An apartment only two miles from an awesome beach where she could surf three or four times a week. She spent her time on things she loved. Her world was utterly in balance.

Well, except for the fact that she had certain physical needs that weren't being met, but you couldn't have everything, right?

Her gaze strayed to Adam. He looked incredible in spite of those silly Hawaiian shorts. And his muscles in that T-shirt—well, *wow*. He wasn't muscle-bound by any means—just the right amount of bulges and sinew, all lean and hearty.

"First stop we have to get you a wet suit. There's a surf shop on the beach. Let's hit it." She locked up her surfboard on a rack outside the shop for that purpose and crooked a finger, motioning him inside.

They entered the surf shop. The lovely smell of waxed boards greeted them. The store was packed with shirtless, barefooted surfer dudes and dudettes. Sand dusted the floor. Ahh, her home away from home. She could spend hours in a surf shop, running her fingers over the boards, inhaling the scent. She got off on surfboards the way some women got off on shoes.

Eva led him to the back of the store where the wet suits were stored. "What size do you wear?"

He told her and she leafed through the offerings. "Since you might not take to surfing, let's go with a lower end model. You can sell it on Craigslist if you decide surfing's not for you."

"Couldn't I just rent one?" he asked.

"You could, but you might really love surfing and the rental fees can add up quickly." She handed him a wet suit and pointed to the dressing room.

"I'm going to look like a dork in this."

"Not at all. But come out and model it for me, I want to make sure it fits you correctly. An ill-fitting wet suit is pure misery."

But when he emerged from the dressing room clad in the wet suit, the misery was all hers as a hard ache yanked up tight in her stomach. Omigosh, the man could have been a swimwear model, he was that hot. The wet suit clung to his honed frame, showcasing every attribute he possessed and he possessed a lot of them.

Eva gulped. She was in over her head with this one. If she was smart, she'd tell him she had a headache and needed to go home. But clearly, she was *not* smart or she wouldn't be here with him in the first place.

"How do I look?" he asked, arms extended.

"Um…"

"That bad, huh?"

No, dammit, that good. "It fits," she mumbled.

"I'll just go change."

"Wear it."

Oh, you shameless hussy. You just want to stare at his ass.

"Just wear it out of the store?"

"No point in changing and then trying to shimmy

into it on the beach," she said, even though she wouldn't have minded watching that, as well.

"Good point."

"Next stop, surfboard rental," she said as they walked up to the cash register to pay for his purchase.

In the process, his elbow brushed lightly against her rib cage, just underneath her breast. She knew the touch was accidental, but that didn't stop her body's red alert.

What if it wasn't accidental?

Eva slid a sideways glance his way as he dug his wallet from the back pocket of the Hawaiian shorts he had thrown over his forearm along with his T-shirt. Neptune himself couldn't have looked sexier.

Okay, so he was sexy. Okay, so she liked him. She wasn't ashamed to admit it. That didn't mean she had to do anything about the attraction.

He was different from the men she was accustomed to—disciplined, logical, handy with a hot water heater. She shivered thinking about how this broad-shouldered man had been in her apartment, so close to her bedroom. Would he be just as handy in bed?

"Cold?" he asked.

Another good quality. Concern for others. *Stop cataloging his good qualities. Look for faults. Look for things that will annoy you after you've dated him for a while.*

Hmm, that was a tall order. She couldn't find anything annoying about him.

"Yeah," she lied.

"Let's get you out in the sun." His smile was genuine, but it seemed rusty, as if he didn't use it often. It wasn't that he was stern, more like he'd forgotten how to play.

Well, she could cure *that*.

You shouldn't be curing anything. You should be keeping your distance. Cure yourself of short-term relationships.

Ah, but honestly, was it so wrong to hang out with him? Maybe she should have a fling with him. Let him be her palette cleanser after Keith. A good guy to restore her faith in human nature.

What would he do if she kissed him right here? A real kiss this time. None of that cheek stuff. Felt that firm mouth on hers. Splayed her fingers over that taut chest; felt his heart skip a beat. Find out if she affected him as strongly as he affected her.

His hand went to the small of her back as he guided her out the door. The slight pressure sent another shiver up her spine. She blinked against the strong sunlight, reality smashing through the sweet little daydream she'd been spinning. Seagulls cawed. A group of college kids played volleyball. The air lay heavy with the scent of sea and sand.

She retrieved her surfboard and they stashed his clothes in a locker. She shimmied into her own wet suit, fully aware that he was watching her from the corner of his eye while trying to pretend that he wasn't. After that, they went to rent a beginner board with a leg rope for him.

They stood in line at the rental kiosk. Amid the middle-aged tourists and their roughhousing kids, Adam looked as out of place as a Hummer in a parking lot full of bicycles.

Really, what kind of accountant had muscles like that? He should have a different career. A bodyguard maybe. Or a military man. He projected that kind of presence. A strong man you could count on. Sure, there was something efficient about him, organized, but he didn't look like the type to sit at a desk all day and crunch numbers.

Once he'd rented the surfboard, she led the way to the beach and even though she was in charge, she couldn't shake the feeling that he was the one guiding things. As if nothing was accidental and he'd orchestrated everything. Where was this feeling coming from?

"What now?" he asked.

"First we wax our boards. You can borrow some of my wax."

"What's the wax for?"

"For traction, so your feet can grip the board. Here, watch me." She laid her board in the sand, pulled a small tin of wax from her beach bag and got down on her knees. Using a circular motion, she demonstrated how to wax it up. "Since you're a beginner, go ahead and wax three-quarters up the length of your board."

He dropped to the sand beside her. He was so close she could smell him. Her nostrils twitched. Damn but he smelled good.

"What next?" he asked when they were finished.

"Stand up." She got to her feet and he followed suit.

"Okay, now wh—" His words were cut off as Eva shoved him in the middle of the back and he stuck out his left foot to catch himself.

"Hey!" Adam scowled. "What did you do that for?"

"Natural footed."

"Huh?"

"I gave you a little shove to see which foot you'd lead with."

"A little warning would have been nice."

"If I'd warned you, it wouldn't have worked. You

would have been thinking about which foot to put first. Determining which foot is dominant requires instinct."

He looked skeptical. "So I'm natural footed, huh?"

"Yes, you lead with your left foot."

"What does that tell me?"

"Where you'll position your feet on the board. You'll put your left foot forward for greater balance."

"Are you natural footed?"

"Nope. I'm a screw."

"Um...*screw?*" Adam said, his face reddening.

He looked so adorably embarrassed that the mischievous imp inside her wanted to chant "screw, screw, screw" just to see what he would do. Did suggestive words fluster him that much? But common sense prevailed and she offered the simple explanation. "Screw-footed, sometimes called goofy-footed after a certain cartoon character who surfed with his right foot forward. Another one of my flaws if you're keeping count. Most people are natural footed."

"Oh." His eyes were on hers, dark and watchful and... *lusty.*

"Are you sure you're an accountant?"

"What?" His eyebrows shot up on his forehead and his mouth rounded.

"Nothing." She waved a hand. "Just an odd thought that passed through my head."

"Do you often express the odd thoughts that pass through your head?"

"All the time." She shook her head, clicked her tongue. "Terrible character flaw."

"Honesty isn't a flaw."

"Ah, so that's what it's called," she teased.

The gleam in his eyes sharpened. "Many people don't appreciate honesty."

"But you do?"

"I do."

"Even when I say 'screw'?" She flirted, knowing she was treading in dangerous territory because she liked the lusty way he was looking at her.

She also liked the way he made her shiver and how her pulse sped up whenever he touched her. She liked how she felt when she was around him—stimulated, fascinated and intrigued. He made her feel special.

He was standing so close, their surfboards side by side in the sand at their feet, their knees almost touching. She could feel the tension in his body. Feel a corresponding tension growing inside her. One small step and her leg would brush against his...

"Eva..."

Her name on his lips came out husky and raw and she'd never been so aroused in the bright sunlight on a public beach. She didn't consciously move. Didn't think about it at all. But her feet, oh, her unruly feet, inched closer, closing the gap between them.

"Yes?"

"What now?" His stare pierced hers, sharp with desire. For her.

My place or yours? she whispered inside her head. Or so she thought.

"Another odd stray thought?"

She slapped a palm over her mouth. "Did I say that out loud? I didn't mean to say that out loud. See what I mean? That terrible character flaw again."

"Honesty is never a terrible thing."

"Meaning?" Tension coiled up tight in her stomach

and her throat and other, more feminine, parts. Her nipples beaded hard, aching to feel his hot tongue.

His gaze flicked downward and the corners of his mouth lifted slightly. That smug little smile caused her nipples to knot even tighter.

"About these surfing lessons…" he said, and stepped away from her.

Eva told herself she was glad he'd backed up, backed off. Relieved. Grateful. Yes, surfing. That's why they'd come here. To teach him to surf and that's what she was going to do, because anything else was pure insanity. She'd learned her lesson. No more jumping headlong into relationships.

But that didn't stop her from wanting to jump his very sexy bones.

ADAM DREADED SURFING.

He was accustomed to being good at what he did and for the most part, in control of his environment. He was a strong swimmer and generally excelled in water sports, but he'd never tried surfing. However, backing out wasn't an option. The fact that he was nervous told him it was something he needed to conquer. Adam didn't believe in letting fear dictate his actions.

So here he was in a wet suit, surfboard under his arm, standing on Del Mar Beach beside Eva. She'd shimmied in her wet suit and he'd been trying his best to keep from noticing how the neoprene conformed to her breasts, but he failed miserably and hadn't heard a word she'd said.

"Adam?"

"Huh?"

"Could you stop staring at my boobs for five minutes

and give me your undivided attention. The last thing I want is for you to drown."

He forced his gaze off her tits and looked her in the eyes. A smile played at her lips. She wasn't the least bit mad at him for ogling her.

"Dude, listen to the lady," said a long-haired beach bum lounging on the sand nearby.

Adam leveled the guy his steeliest military officer's glare. The guy raised his palms and then went back to waxing his surfboard.

"I'm listening," Adam told Eva.

What a lie. His ears were attuned to the sounds of her sexy breathing, not what she was saying.

You can handle this. You're strong. You're athletic. Who won MVP on your high school baseball team?

His athleticism might help with the surfing, but how was he going to justify the erection straining against his wet suit? He needed to get into the water now before he embarrassed himself again.

"Got it," he said. "Let's hit the water."

He turned his board to hide what he didn't want her to see—a repeat of what had happened in yoga class—and struck out for the water.

Look what the woman had done to him. She was going to think he was a first-class perv. He found it damned disturbing. The water splashed cool against his ankles and he was happy for the distraction, but unfortunately it did nothing to dash his rising libido when she came running up alongside him.

"Let's go over the basics again," she said, summing up what she'd just taught him.

He tried to process it, but there was so much to learn. All this time he'd thought surfing was a lawless free-for-all without structure or rules when nothing was further from the truth. He liked the discipline of it, but hated being in over his head.

"Grip your board like this," she hollered over the sound of the waves, demonstrating the technique.

Focus on surfing, he lectured himself, mimicking her movements and gliding into the water on his board. Higgins had told him to hang out with her, watch over her and pry as much info as he could from her about Barksdale. That did not include getting all hot and horny over his target.

He'd never been this out of his element before, both in the surf and in this thing with Eva. If he was smart, he'd call Higgins and tell him that he needed to put someone else on the assignment, that he couldn't handle himself.

Yes, that would look so professional. And what about redeeming yourself? What about catching Barksdale so he didn't have to feel so ashamed for letting the theft happen in the first place?

Because he did feel responsible, even though he'd followed every protocol and done everything he could to keep the data safe. Barksdale had simply been better than Navy Intelligence. And there was the rub. Adam's division was supposed to be the best of the best and they couldn't stop a civilian computer hacker from stealing top secret government documents. Even though no one blamed him, he blamed himself. He'd failed. And failure wasn't something Adam swallowed easily.

"Here comes a nice mushy beginner's wave," Eva called out. "Get ready to use the stance I showed you."

Stance. Right. The one he hadn't been paying attention to because he'd been too busy ogling her.

A slow rolling wave came toward them, frothy white and gentle. Girly wave.

"Put your hands under your chest and raise up. Like cobra pose in yoga class."

Sure. He'd get right on that.

"Push up from your hands and toes," Eva hollered as the wave reached them.

He did as she said and suddenly he was up, teetering on the board.

"Bring your right foot back, left foot forward."

For a moment he thought he was going into the ocean headfirst, but somehow he managed to get the correct stance, bend his knees, and extend his arms for balance.

"Look forward, eyes straight ahead, chin up."

That was no problem. His military training kicked in and the next thing he knew, Adam was surfing. Okay, yeah, it was the kiddie version of surfing, but he was up on the board and balanced and a wave was rolling underneath him.

It felt like playful sex. Fun and easy.

Eva was on her surfboard beside him, gliding effortlessly along. "Hey, you're a natural."

He grinned and for the first time in a long time, he felt truly free. And then he went and spoiled it all by losing his focus and shifting his gaze to stare at her sexy body in the wet suit and bam! Right into the water he fell.

Luckily she'd leashed his board to his ankle with the ankle rope. Otherwise it would have been lost in the waves. He managed to get turned around and back on the board. His legs were already feeling rubbery—this from a guy who ran three miles a day—and he spat out a mouthful of salty seawater.

But even so, he couldn't stop imagining what she would look like without that wet suit on, surfing naked like Neptune's nymph. He wondered if she had ever surfed nude. He'd bet hard money on it and Adam was not a betting man.

Dammit! He had to stop this.

He lay belly down on the board and let the waves push him back to shore.

"Where are you going?" Eva called. "We're just getting started."

No, ma'am, he was done. No way was he going to be able to keep his erection in check as long as she was wearing that skintight suit. Not even the cold Pacific Ocean could take the starch out of his...er...*sail.*

"I need a break," he said.

"Okay." She nodded. "I'm going to paddle on out and see if I can catch some bigger waves."

No, wait. He'd thought she'd come back to shore with him. He didn't want her going off on her own, far away from him.

Already she was gone, swimming off on her board, out of earshot.

Dammit. He paddled after her, getting sloshed and tossed by waves. Gritting his teeth, he barreled ahead. He was not letting her out of his sight.

But the same currents that were carrying her out to sea, seemed to be shoving his surfboard toward the shore. Water had gotten into his ears—why hadn't he thought to wear earplugs—and he couldn't hear anything but the whooshing noise of the ocean and his own quickening heartbeat.

Every time the wave lifted him up, he searched for her. She was several hundred yards away. Other surfers paddled near her. A sailboat skimmed the horizon. And there was a Jet Ski out in open waters, moving fast toward Eva.

Uneasiness washed over him. He didn't like this position of weakness, not one damned bit.

Up he went on the wave, saw the Jet Ski pulling up beside her. Salt water stung his eyes and it was hard to see. His gut went cold. Something didn't feel right. Was she in trouble? Had the Jet Ski rider stopped to help her? Or was there another more nefarious explanation? Could it be Barksdale?

He didn't know where that thought came from, but it spurred him into action. The surfboard was an encumbrance, getting in his way. He had to shed it.

Adam reached down, stripped off the ankle rope, let go of the board and went after her, swimming against the tide with all his might.

10

EVA WAS GETTING READY to curl a beautiful wave when a Jet Ski zoomed up, sending her tumbling for a loop. She came up sputtering and glaring, prepared to tongue-lash the jerk for getting too close. She grabbed her board and swiped her hair from her eyes and looked up to see a man staring down at her.

An unpleasant jolt of recognition went through her. Keith. "Thanks a lot for the dowsing."

He didn't look the least bit contrite. "Sorry."

"What in the hell were you thinking?"

"I was out jumping the waves, saw you and came over to say hi."

She gripped the board tightly. "Hi, now goodbye."

The waves tossed him closer to her. She did not want to be close to this man. Just looking at him made her ache for a hot shower. Yes, he was good-looking, but he was also a criminal and she'd stupidly dated him.

"I've been trying to call you," he said. "Left a message. You didn't call me back."

"Are you shocked about that? Considering you left me holding the bag with the Navy. They took me down for questioning."

"What did you tell them?"

"I had nothing to tell them other than obviously I didn't know you at all if you'd steal from your own country. What did you steal?"

"Innocent until proven guilty," Keith said. "But that's what I wanted to talk to you about. To apologize."

"Apology accepted. Now go away." She made a shooing motion.

"Who's the guy you've been hanging out with?" Keith jerked his chin in the direction of the beach.

"Don't tell me you're jealous." She snorted. "You get no say in who I date."

"He doesn't look like your type."

"Wait a minute, how do you know I've been hanging out with anyone?"

"I've been waiting for a chance to talk to you."

A prick of fear pierced her. "Have you been following me?"

"I needed to see you."

"That's stalking, Keith. There are laws against it. And might I remind you that you're the one who broke up with me. Not that it really bothered me. I deserve so much better than you."

"Listen—"

"So you've been following me and the best place you could find to talk to me is the middle of the ocean? What's wrong with coming to my apartment?"

"They can't bug the ocean."

"Who?"

"The Navy."

Alarmed, she asked, "Keith, just what in the hell did you do?"

The wind buffeted his Jet Ski even closer to her. She pushed away, disgusted with herself for having struck up a romance with him. God, what had she been thinking?

That was it. She hadn't been thinking. She'd just been out for a good time and look where it had gotten her. She just wanted to get back to Adam—

Adam. She'd been so creeped out by Keith that she'd forgotten about Adam. Where was he?

Ignoring Keith, she turned in the water, scanning toward the shore, and finally spied him several yards away giving the distress signal.

Crap! He was in trouble.

She turned back to Keith to ask him to take the Jet Ski over to Adam and help, but Keith was already speeding away.

Fine. Right. Worthless ass.

Resolutely, she launched herself on her board and headed toward Adam.

She caught a wave and it only took her a couple of minutes to reach him, but the journey seemed forever. He kept going down under the waves and each time, she feared he wouldn't come back up, but thankfully, he held on.

"Where's your board?" she gasped as soon as she reached him. His eyes were bloodshot, his face pale, his lips tinged blue. He looked exhausted.

"Took it off to come after you."

"What did you do that for?" she asked, extending her board to him so they could both hang on.

"I thought you were in trouble. That Jet Ski came up on you and I—"

"I was fine."

"How was I to know that?"

"You thought I was in trouble and you came after

me?" She felt a tugging in the center of her chest. A sweet, sappy, dangerous feeling.

"The guy on the Jet Ski—"

"My old boyfriend. The creep I told you about."

Adam turned his head to look at the departing Jet Ski that was now far in the distance. He scowled and his eyes clouded.

Aww, was he jealous? The tugging in her chest intensified.

"What did he want? Did he threaten you? Hurt you?"

She shook her head. "No, no, he just wanted to talk to me."

"About what?"

Okay, that was officially none of his business. Jealousy might be cute. Possessiveness was not. Especially since she and Adam didn't even have a relationship going.

"I don't have to answer that."

"Do you still have feelings for him?"

Eva scowled. "What do you care?"

"I don't. It's just…" He looked like he was about to say something else and then he clenched his jaw shut.

"Yes?"

"Never mind."

"If you have something to say to me, just spit it out."

"What did he want?"

She wasn't going to tell him that Keith had just dropped by in the middle of the ocean to tell her that the Navy could very well be bugging her apartment. She was still trying to process that and how would it look to Adam if he learned she'd been mixed up with a guy who was in serious trouble with the Navy?

"I've got nothing to say."

Well, that was that. Nothing to do now but head back to shore and try to figure out what had just passed between them.

They clung to the board, kicking in unison, heading back toward the beach. She was so aware of him. The water and waves and sun retreated into the background until he encompassed everything.

He'd thought she was in trouble and he'd come out to help her. And he was jealous of Keith. She tried not to smile, but she couldn't help it.

"What are you grinning about?" he growled.

"You."

"I amuse you?"

"Yeah, you do."

"Never had a jealous boyfriend before?"

"You're not my boyfriend."

"My loss."

She startled, turning to stare at him. His face was right next to hers, his dark eyes dilated. From sun, she told herself, but feared it was from something else. Something far more complicated.

Relief rushed through her when her feet touched sand. She stood up, Adam following suit.

"We're here," she said, the surfboard still between them.

"Yeah."

His eyes never strayed from her face, leaving Eva to wonder just where "here" was.

THEY COLLAPSED ONTO THE SAND where Eva had left her beach bag, both of them winded and exhausted. Adam lay on his back, staring up at the cloudless blue sky, while Eva rolled over on her stomach and rested her face in the crook of her arm.

He was trying to figure out exactly what had happened out there. Not just between him and Eva, but between Eva and Barksdale. Had it been a planned rendezvous with Barksdale that he'd inadvertently inserted himself into? Could she actually be in on it with Barksdale?

The thought chilled his blood. Higgins didn't think she was involved. But there were some cool customers out there; was she much more devious than she seemed?

Adam shot a glance over at her. Her breath was coming out in soft chuffs, her face hidden from him. Right now, he had the strongest urge to roll her over and kiss her. Never mind that they were both short of breath from exertion. Never mind they were on a public beach where everyone could see. Never mind that he now had worrisome suspicions about her true relationship with Barksdale. His mouth burned with the overwhelming urge to taste hers.

He shouldn't be having these thoughts. He should be getting to his cell phone, calling Higgins, telling him about Barksdale on the Jet Ski. But what was the rush? Barksdale was long gone and Eva was right here, warm and womanly and safe with him.

Adam sat up, prepared to throw away all common sense, commit a tactical error, grab her by her shoulders, flip her over and just kiss her to see if she really did taste like sunshine.

Eva turned just as he leaned over her. She raised her head and crashed solidly into his jaw.

"Oww!" they yelled in unison. He clutched his chin while she pressed a hand to the crown of her head.

"What were you doing?" She glowered at him.

"I was leaning over to kiss you."

"Seriously? I thought we just had a fight."

"We didn't have a fight. We just groused at each other."

"And that puts you in the mood for kissing?"

"No, lying next to you in the sand puts me in the mood for kissing."

"I thought we had an agreement. Just friends."

"I want to renegotiate the terms."

"Even now? After I whacked you in the chin?"

He rubbed his jaw. "I've worked with worse handicaps."

She moved in closer, parted her lips.

He lowered his head. They hovered there, staring into each other's eyes. He put his arm around her waist, pulled her close. He wanted to make this the best kiss he'd ever given anyone. He wanted her toes to curl.

Eva chuckled. "Hurry and kiss me already. The suspense is killing me."

"You're making fun," he said.

"You're too meticulous. Stop thinking and just do it before there's no chance that the kiss will live up to the anticipation."

He glanced down at where he and Eva sat with their arms entangled around each other. Eva had thrown her head back and her laughter circled the air along with the seagulls. Sand covered his body and his toes and fingers were wrinkly from the water. He tasted ocean, smelled hot dogs cooking from a vendor down the beach and he realized something startling. He was happy. Truly happy in a way he hadn't been since he was a kid.

"Adam? Adam Mancuso? Is that you?"

He jerked his gaze upward and spied a woman coming toward them.

No way! It couldn't be. What was this? Attack of the exes? Running into Eva's old boyfriend and his former fiancée all in the same day? It felt too unbelievable. Especially when as far as he knew, Kirsten still lived in Maryland.

Eva peered over. At some point when they'd been in the ocean, the band had come loose from her ponytail and now her hair was plastered wetly to her head. Adam thought she looked like a sexy mermaid—tousled and windblown—but Eva was quickly combing her fingers through the tresses, trying to tame her tangled locks.

Kirsten, looking elegant in a dark blue one-piece suit, sauntered over. She pushed her sunglasses up on her forehead, shaded her eyes with her hand and squinted at him. She had always been a touch nearsighted.

Adam scrambled to his feet, dusting sand from his knees, springing away from Eva. "K-Kirsten," he stammered. "What are you doing here?"

"I could ask you the same thing."

"Um…I'm surfing." He was feeling like he'd felt when he was a kid in school and the teacher caught him standing outside of the lunch line. He halfway expected her to snap her fingers and say, "Get back in line."

"I can see that." She raised an eyebrow. "But why?"

"Why am I surfing or why am I in San Diego?" He shifted his weight, swung his hands. He was aware of the heat of Eva's gaze from behind him.

"Either one. Both."

"Just having fun." He gestured at Eva's surfboard parked on the sand. His rental board was MIA. That was going to cost him his deposit.

Kirsten's jaw unhinged. "You? Just having fun?"

"Why not?" He smiled.

"And smiling. You're smiling."

He shrugged. "I suppose I am."

"This is revolutionary."

He held his arms wide. "The new me."

Kirsten ran an assessing gaze over him. "Well, it looks good on you."

He suddenly realized all the problems Kirsten could cause him if the conversation continued. She could let it slip that he was no accountant. That he worked for the ONI. Anxiety set in, but Adam had been trained to control his emotions. Calm under pressure.

"You're looking good, Kirsten," he said, intentionally lowering his voice, giving her a compliment so she'd be flattered and stop talking about him.

Her face pinkened with delight. "Flattery as well from my stoic old flame. Will miracles never cease? What has gotten into you? Whatever it is, I like it."

"Hi!" Eva came around from behind him, her hand fully extended. "I'm Eva. The thing that's gotten into your stoic old flame."

Adam cringed outwardly, but inwardly, a small part of him was pleased. Eva was just as jealous of Kirsten as he'd been over Barksdale.

"Oh, well, hello…" Kirsten shook Eva's sandy hand. "It's great to meet you."

"You, too." Eva's smile was as sweet as dill pickles.

"So…surfing." Kirsten dropped Eva's hand and shifted her gaze back to Adam.

"Yeah, surfing." He was trying to send Kirsten a message with his eyes, begging her not to mention what he did for a living, but she wasn't getting the hint.

She met his gaze and he saw a longing in them that he

hadn't seen since they were first dating. Crap! Kirsten wanted him.

"Remember when I tried to get you to go inline skating with me?"

"Um-hmm."

"And snow skiing."

"Yep, yep." He plastered a palm to the back of his neck.

"You were always too busy. Not interested. The only thing you'd ever do was play golf, go running or work out at the gym and that was only because it helped you in your job or kept you in shape."

"Bad, bad boyfriend."

"Not bad," she contradicted. "Just not much fun."

"I can see why you left me. It's been nice catching up..."

"But now look at him," Eva said. "He's surfing with me. And yoga. He takes my yoga classes. You should see his sacral chakra. Out of this world red."

"Seriously?" Kirsten gawked. "You take yoga?"

Sheepishly, Adam raised his palms in an I-surrender gesture. What was it going to take to move Kirsten along?

"Honey! There you are."

They all turned to see a man coming up the beach carrying two Italian ices. His haircut looked expensive though oddly enough, not a hair moved in the ocean breeze. He had on, of all things, a sweater tied around his neck by the sleeves and an orangey tan that looked as if it came from a bottle. The guy was the epitome of an Ivy League prepster. Right up Kirsten's alley.

"Hey." The guy's grin was all teeth.

"Hey," Eva responded.

"My fiancé," Kirsten explained. "Teddy, this is Adam and Eva."

"Now that's just plain funny." Teddy chortled. "Adam and Eva."

What a douche. Adam knew he hadn't been much fun when he'd been with Kirsten. He'd kept his mind fully focused on proving himself in the ONI. He knew his single-mindedness had been a large part of what had killed them as a couple, but holy hand grenade, he never expected her to dump him for Malibu boy.

"Wait a minute," Teddy said, passing one of the Italian ices to Kirsten. "Are you *Adam,* Adam?"

He wanted to quip, "The one and only." But since he wasn't much of a quipper, he said instead, "That'd be me."

"I was just telling Adam I couldn't believe he was surfing." The wind whipped a strand of hair in Kirsten's mouth and she tugged it out with an index finger painted a glossy pink. Adam couldn't help comparing her sleek manicure to Eva's short trimmed nails.

Kirsten's mouth produced a pout. "He never used to do anything fun."

Eva slipped an arm around his waist. "That certainly doesn't sound like the Adam I know. Around me he's all about fun, fun, fun."

He almost grinned at that, but managed to keep a straight face. He needed to get out of this situation ASAP before the conversation got around to what he did for a living.

"*Real*-ly?" Kirsten drawled out the word as if she didn't believe it.

Eva slung her arm over his shoulders, pulling him closer to her. "Really."

"Well, then, I'm so happy—I never thought he'd ever loosen up."

"Oh, he's loose all right." Eva winked. "If you know what I mean."

Kirsten's eyes widened and her mouth narrowed into disapproval. Good, Eva had pissed her off. Maybe now she and Malibu boy would wander off down the beach with their Italian ices.

But instead, Kirsten said, "Since you've turned over a new leaf, Adam, I have a brilliant idea. You know why I'm in town don't you?"

"Um…" Adam stalled. He didn't have a clue.

"It's the annual Shady Palms Charity Scramble." To Eva she said, "The proceeds go to fight cystic fibrosis. My baby sister died of C.F., so I play in the tournament every year. Adam's even played with me. It's a night scramble so that's always a lot of fun."

Oh, yeah, he'd forgotten about that. He'd played in the tournament once during the three years they'd been together. Work had prevented him from joining her on the other occasions.

"Here's the thing," Kirsten said. "If we don't find a decent couple to join us, we're going to be stuck with this geriatric duo. We really could use you on our team, Adam." She said his name like she had honey stuck to the roof of her mouth and she was licking it off.

"I…"

He grappled for a good excuse not to join them, but before he could come up with one, Eva said, "We'd love to!"

Kirsten cast a glance over at Eva. "You know how to golf?"

"I've knocked a few balls around at a munici-pal course, nothing like Shady Palms, but I'm game for anything." Eva poked Adam in the ribs. "Right, honey?"

"Er...um..." Adam stammered.

"You're on," Kirsten said. "Since it's a scramble we can take up the slack if you're unable to produce."

"You won't have to take up any slack from me."

"We'll see." Kirsten smirked. "I'm so glad we ran into you. This is going to be such fun. See you there tomorrow evening at eight."

"Ah, dammit," Adam said. "We can't. Sorry. Eva has a yoga class to teach."

"I can switch classes with one of the other women at the studio," Eva said. "I wouldn't miss this for the world."

"OKAY," EVA SAID THE MINUTE Kirsten and Teddy had walked away. "That woman has a serious bug up her butt. Count yourself lucky she dumped you for Malibu boy."

"Malibu boy." Adam laughed. "That's exactly what I was calling him in my head."

"Seriously, that hair! How did he get it to stay so perfectly in place? Aqua Net?"

"My guess is he doesn't set a toe in the water."

"Of course not. There are creatures in the water," Eva mocked.

"You're bad."

"You had any doubts about that?"

"None at all, but I wish you hadn't got us into this golf scramble thing. Why did you get us into it?"

Eva shrugged. "I guess I was jealous."

"Jealous? Of Kirsten? Sunshine, you've got it all over her, in spades."

Sunshine.

The word was a caress to her ears. Adam wasn't the type to toss endearments around lightly.

"She thinks I'm your girlfriend."

"Well, you did lead her to that impression. Throwing your arm around me and all."

"She was looking at you like you were the last pork chop on the plate and she'd been on a cabbage soup diet for two weeks."

Adam laughed again and the hearty sound warmed her from the inside out. He thought she was cute and funny. "Poor Malibu boy."

Eva grinned. "You have a great laugh. You should use it more often."

"I'll keep that in mind."

"So," she said, "you think you can give me a crash course in golfing? I've never played a day in my life."

_11_

"WE DON'T HAVE TO PLAY GOLF with them," Adam said when they were back in the Jeep heading home.

"No," she said, "I want to."

"Why would you want to do that?"

"I taught you to surf, you can teach me to golf."

"I can do that without having to play a scramble with my ex-girlfriend and her helmet-haired fiancé."

"It's for charity."

"What's the real reason?" he probed.

"I dunno." Eva shrugged. "Why do you think she asked?"

"You think she's trying to win me back?"

"You don't have to smirk about it. I'm no more jealous of Kirsten than you are of Keith."

She had a point, but he couldn't tell her the real reason he was so concerned about Barksdale. "He came after you on a Jet Ski."

"He's hardly a white knight on a shining stead."

"No unresolved feelings?" He didn't want to hear it if there was, but he pushed. Because of his job.

"Keith means nothing to me. He was a passing thing."

"Kirsten doesn't mean anything to me, either."

"Of course she does. You were engaged to her. Honestly, I'm not jealous. I just want to see you in your milieu. So far, we've been on my turf. Yoga studio, the beach."

"I thought you said we weren't dating. That we were just friends."

She stopped at a traffic light and turned her head to stare him straight in the eyes. "I think we both know that's impossible."

Oh, shit. She was right. And this couldn't be happening at a worse time. But a part of him—the reckless, impulsive part that he hadn't even known existed until he'd been assigned to watch over her—wanted to gather his smart little Eva in his arms right here and kiss her until she couldn't breathe.

But then his sense of honor took over. How could he have a sexual relationship with a target? It went against all protocol. It could even get him thrown out of the Navy. He was walking on a razor's edge. One wrong move and he'd get cut.

Or worse, cut Eva.

He had to back off. Keep his desire in check. At least until the assignment was over.

And then after that?

Which raised another question. Once she found out that he'd been sent to spy on her, would she ever speak to him? The idea of her not ever speaking to him again shouldn't have him feeling so wretched. He'd only known her a week, but there it was. He couldn't change it.

When they arrived back at their apartment complex, he hopped out and grabbed hold of her surfboard, determined to carry it upstairs for her.

She sank her hands on her hips. "I'm not helpless, you know."

"Never said you were." He moved past her, caught a whiff of sweet scent and had to fight off his instincts again. God, how he wanted to kiss her.

He stopped when he got to her door. She came up behind him, keys in hand. She'd taken off her wet suit at the beach and wore only her bikini top and shorts. The blue butterfly tattoo was highly visible in the sunlight. He ached to press his lips to that butterfly, taste the salty tang of her skin.

"So," she said.

"So," he echoed.

"See you tomorrow evening?"

He nodded.

She gave him one last smile—how had he lived before he'd seen her smile?—and closed the door.

Leaving Adam to make his way back to his apartment, his heart staggering around in his chest like a Mardi Gras drunk. If Commander Higgins had him hooked up to a polygraph machine and asked him about his feelings for Eva, there's no way he could lie and get away with it. She stirred his blood, burned his brain, drove him crazy in a way no woman ever had. And crazy was not a healthy state of mind for a naval intelligence officer.

Once inside his apartment, he made the call to Commander Higgins and told him about what had happened in the ocean.

"So Barksdale is definitely still in San Diego." Higgins sounded relieved. "Good work, Mancuso. This lets me know my theory is correct. St. George is the key. This was the development we needed. I'm calling the judge to see if he'll give us permission to tap her phone lines now. Did you find out what Barksdale said to her?"

"She didn't want to talk about it and I couldn't insist without looking suspicious."

"You're a smart guy, Adam. Find a way to get her to open up to you."

"About that, sir. I'm not sure I'm the man for this job. I'm afraid I'm losing my objectivity when it comes to Eva...er...the target."

"You've already made inroads with this woman. She trusts you."

Yeah and I'm going to hurt her just like Barksdale did and that'll crush her. "You could just bring her in for questioning again."

"Let's save that as an option of last resort in the off chance that she is involved. We can't afford to tip our hand. You can do this, Lieutenant. It's why I selected you for this detail. You've always been able to separate your heart from your head."

He had. Until now. Until Eva.

"Find out what Barksdale discussed with your target. And that's an order, sailor."

Dork.

Eva had never felt more out of her element as she stared at herself in the mirror of the pro shop dressing room at the Shady Palms Country Club.

They'd arranged to meet the other couple at the country club, and the minute Kirsten had seen Eva in her pair of cutoff blue jeans and a tank top, she'd grabbed her by the hand and whisked her into the shop.

"We'll get you properly attired," she'd said, and flashed her Mastercard. "My treat."

"I can't let you pay for this," Eva protested.

"Sure you can. You can't go on the course dressed like you're going to wash a car."

"Why not? It'll be dark out soon. No one will be able to see me."

"Shady Palms is one of the most exclusive country clubs in Southern California. This charity is a big deal. Local television stations cover this event."

"Why didn't you say so?" Eva said, feeling embarrassed. "I can pay for my own clothes."

Kirsten looked at her. "You're a what? Size eight?"

"Six."

"*Real*-ly? You look like an eight."

"Six," Eva said through clenched teeth.

"Here. Try these." Kirsten had jammed a handful of golfing outfits in her arms and sent her into the dressing room.

Now she was standing here in a short little pink-and-white skirt and polo shirt with a matching visor, golfing shoes with cleats and pink sports socks with fuzzy pompoms, looking all the world like Lovey Howell from *Gilligan's Island*.

"Do you think the cleats are really necessary?" she asked Kirsten. "I mean most likely this is the only time I'll be playing golf."

"If you're with Adam, you'll be playing a lot of golf," Kirsten said. "That is if you want to spend any time with him at all. There are only two things he cares about and that's his work and golf."

"He's taking my yoga class and he came surfing with me," Eva pointed out.

"That was just to get you in bed. You know how men are."

It was probably just Kirsten being petty, but the comment hit Eva like a rock. She didn't belong with the country club set. She was the daughter of a hairdresser from Cut and Shoot, Texas. A woman who'd learned early on that if you put a big smile on your face no one would guess how lonely you were inside. Not only that, but if you kept your attachments loosely tied, it wouldn't hurt so much when the threads broke.

Now here she was being stuffed into a Stepford Wife costume. This role of well-heeled hottie didn't fit. It never would. And if that's what Adam wanted, well then...

No, this was dumb. Spending money on an outfit she would never, ever wear again, or even worse, letting Adam's ex-fiancée buy it for her. If Zoey was here she'd probably tell her to let Kirsten fork over the cash, but she wasn't as brash as Zoey. Besides, Eva had too much pride for that.

She looked at the price tag dangling from the sleeve and almost choked. The shirt alone cost more than she made in a day.

"You better get used to spending that kind of money if you're going to be dating Senator Orin Mancuso's son."

"What?"

"Adam's dad is a senator. You didn't know?"

Eva shook her head.

"Maryland State."

"I had no idea."

"I'm not surprised he hasn't told you. He doesn't like flaunting his family money."

Eva's knees went weak. She had no business entertaining romantic thoughts about a senator's son. None at all. "He's wealthy?"

"Not Donald Trump wealthy, but yes, the Mancusos are quite well-off."

Eva gulped. If he had megabucks, why was Adam slumming in her modest apartment complex? "You know, maybe it's better if I don't play in this scramble with you guys."

The gleam in Kirsten's eyes told her that's exactly what she'd been angling for all along. Eva wondered why the woman had invited her to the scramble. Had it been too much to hope that she'd just wanted to be nice?

There you go again, trusting people when you shouldn't.

Now she could see the other woman's ulterior motive. Kirsten wanted to show Eva up as an unsophisticated surfer girl not worthy of a Mancuso. Was she trying to get Adam back? Was that really what was going on here? What about her new fiancé, Malibu boy…er…Teddy.

"You know what?" Eva said. "Screw the cost. I'll take the outfit."

WHEN KIRSTEN STEPPED FROM the pro shop with Eva, Adam snagged his ex-fiancée by the elbow. "Could I speak with you in private?"

It had been his intention to intercept Kirsten as soon as they arrived and tell her to keep quiet about his job, but before he'd had a chance to do that, she'd commandeered Eva and hustled her into the store. He was already on edge. Higgins had called him that afternoon and told him he'd gotten the warrant for a wiretap on Eva's phones. He was to place a listening device in her cell, while Rogers and Kilgore tapped her home phone. He hated having to violate her privacy this way.

Kirsten's eyes widened. "Sure, sure. Teddy, could you take Eva with you to get our carts?"

Teddy scowled as if he didn't much like the idea, but he held his arm out to Eva.

Eva, who looked amazing in a short pink skirt, tossed a glance at him over her shoulder. Adam smiled reassuringly at her. "This won't take a minute."

He dragged Kirsten off to one side as carts loaded with golfers headed for the greens. Many were already on the lighted course whacking around glowing green golf balls.

"Look," he said. "There's something I have to tell you about Eva."

"You're crazy about her," Kirsten said flatly.

Adam was startled. "What? No."

"It's written all over you."

Unwilling to deal with that comment, he shoved it aside. "Did you tell her anything about me?"

"I told her you were rich."

Adam shifted nervously. "How did she react?"

"She looked panicked. She's out of her league with you and she knows it."

That pissed him off. "Eva can hold her own with anyone."

"What would your parents think of her? A tattoo on her shoulder? How tacky."

He wanted to give Kirsten's arm a good shake and tell her to stop judging Eva, but he held his temper. "Did you tell her I was with the ONI?"

"You haven't told her that yet?"

"I can't. She's my target."

Kirsten's eyes widened. "She's an assignment?"

Adam blew out his breath and plastered a palm to the nape of his neck. "Yeah."

"Ah, that explains a lot. For a minute there I wasn't getting the connection. Why you'd be dating someone like her."

"Don't you dare denigrate Eva. She's a wonderful person. Kind and generous and funny and—"

"You have fallen for her." Kirsten clicked her tongue. "You are so screwed. When she finds out you've been spying on her, lying to her. And what's your C.O. going to say?"

Adam shoved his palm over his head. "Yeah, I know."

"It wouldn't have worked out anyway."

"What do you mean?"

"You two…" Kirsten wrinkled her nose. "I don't see it. Not long term, anyway."

"Why not?" he challenged.

"Besides the fact you're investigating her?"

He wasn't really investigating Eva, more like protecting her, but he didn't bother enlightening Kirsten to the difference. "Yeah."

"You're so opposite. Night and day."

"Opposites attract."

"Up to a point. Maybe. But it will only last if your values are similar. Are your values similar?"

Hell if he knew.

Kirsten must have read his doubt on his face. "You haven't even talked about the important things, have you?"

"Not in so many words."

She shook her head. "You haven't changed in that respect. You never were much of a talker. Lord knows I tried to get you to tell me what was going on in that thick skull of yours."

"I'm talking now."

"About another woman. You never wanted to talk about us."

"You say Eva and I are too dissimilar to make it—"

"You two are like a peanut butter and sausage sandwich. Nothing goes together."

"Well, you and I were too much alike. Peanut butter and jelly gets damned boring."

"Now you're just being mean." Her tone turned frosty.

"You were bored with me, too." He jerked his head in Teddy's direction. "Is he more than just a plaything?"

"We're engaged."

"Because you have similar values."

"Yes. We both want the same things from life. Do you and yoga girl? Oh, wait. I forgot. You haven't talked. I'm sure you've been spending too much time surfing and sexing it up for that."

"Why yes," Adam said, knowing he sounded malicious but not caring at this point. He wasn't going to let Kirsten malign Eva. "She sure knows how to sex me up."

"You're saying I didn't?"

He shrugged.

Kirsten's eyes flashed fire.

"Okay," he apologized. "That wasn't fair. What we had was nice—"

"Yes, just nice and for the record, Teddy is excellent in bed."

"Good for you."

"Honey," Teddy called out. "It's our tee time."

"Good luck," Kirsten muttered to Adam. "You're going to need it."

"Please don't say anything to Eva about what I do."

"Don't worry. I'll leave that shocking little surprise to you."

12

FEELING A BIT DAZED, Eva followed Teddy to pick up their golf carts. They threaded their way around camera crews and celebrities who'd shown up to play in the charity event.

As much as she hated to admit it, she was glad Kirsten had forced her to buy a golfing outfit. At least she didn't stick out like the proverbial sore thumb. Dusk was starting to gather and Eva was delighted to notice the golf balls glowed in the dark. How fun.

That was the way to get through this thing, just have fun and not worry too much about what anyone thought. That attitude had served her well for most of her life. Heck, this was for charity after all.

Teddy showed her where to sign in. He wasn't such a bad sort, once you got past the hair and the superwhite teeth and the fake tan and the sweater.

She got out her purse to pay the—*yikes*—two hundred dollar entry fee only to be told her fee had already been covered by Adam Mancuso. That embarrassed her. Why was everyone trying to pay her way? Did she come across as that broke? Sure, she wasn't rolling in dough, but she could cough up two hundred dollars for a good cause.

On top of the new golfing outfit?

Okay, yes, she'd have to eat ramen noodles for the rest of the month, but she'd blown money on more frivolous things. Just because Adam had money didn't mean she was going to let him pay her way. She'd tell him that as soon as he showed up.

Their foursome had been assigned a caddy, and Eva was surprised to discover it was a ruddy-face middle-aged woman.

"Hi," she said, extending her hand to Eva. "I'm Patti Carson, your caddy."

"Nice to meet you. I'm Eva. How long have you been a caddy?"

"Oh, aren't you the cutest thing. I'm not really a caddy. My husband manages Shady Palms, I'm just helping out with the event."

Eva liked Patti immediately. She wasn't at all pretentious as she'd imagined exclusive country club types would be.

"Where's your clubs?" Patti asked.

"Um…" Clubs. Why hadn't she thought about clubs?

"Here are our clubs," Adam said. He was dressed in tan slacks and a sapphire-blue polo shirt, looking collegiate and moneyed, and carrying a pink golf bag in one hand with brand-new shiny clubs and a used set in a black bag.

"You bought me golf clubs?" Eva stared at him in disbelief.

"Did you have a set of your own?"

She swallowed as if she had a hunk of bread caught in her throat. Who was this man? "No, but—"

"Now you do."

"Adam, I can't accept these. They must have cost hundreds of dollars."

"My gift to you."

"It's too extravagant."

"You need something to play with."

She leaned close to him. "You know I don't know how to play."

"I'm hoping that after tonight you'll fall in love with the game."

Why was that? She met his gaze. A small, vulnerable smile tipped his lips. Did this mean he wanted her to learn how to play golf so they could play together? Her heart did a backflip.

Do not get ahead of yourself.

"Please accept," Adam said. "Let me do something nice for you.

"Thank you," she said finally because she really didn't have much of a choice. How was she going to play golf without clubs? She'd idiotically thought she would be able to rent some the way you rented shoes at the bowling alley. Yeah, boy, around this crowd she felt as sophisticated as homemade soap.

"You're welcome."

"It's a very generous gift, also considering you paid for my entry fee. Especially since it's all my fault I got us into this."

"Don't sweat it." Adam turned to load the bags in the caddy cart.

"Your boyfriend is very sweet," Patti whispered to Eva. "And I do appreciate him loading those bags for me. You wouldn't believe how many men would just leave it to me."

"Oh, he's not my boyfriend. We're just friends."

Patti arched an eyebrow, smiled. "Does he know that?"

"What do you mean?"

"The way he looks at you." Patti shook her head. "That man has more than just friendship in mind."

Was it that obvious? Eva peeked over at Adam, only to catch him studying her speculatively. She ducked her head, glanced away.

"Ready?" Adam asked, coming over to hold out his hand to her.

As if she needed help getting into a golf cart. She pretended she didn't see his hand—the sexual tension was acute enough without touching him—and slid across the seat of the golf cart.

They followed Teddy and Kirsten, who'd already struck out for the first tee. Patti followed behind them in her cart laden with everyone's clubs. The sun was hanging on the horizon and the high-powered lamps around the greens started to come on. Fireflies flicked through the trees and the air smelled of fresh mown grass.

"Relax," Adam said. "You're going to do fine."

"Who says I'm not relaxed."

"The way you're gripping the seat. Your knuckles are white."

"That's a bit of a switch," she said. "*You* telling *me* to relax."

"You give good advice, I'm handing it back to you."

"It's hard not to be nervous when I'm around all these rich people and celebrities. I had no idea it was going to be like this. I had no idea *you* were rich. How come you didn't tell me that you were rich?"

"My family is rich. I just make a regular salary."

"A salary good enough to pay for my entry fee and a set of golf clubs."

"You sound angry with me."

"I feel blindsided. Why is a guy like you living in an apartment complex like mine?"

He shrugged. "*Our* apartment complex is nice."

"Not that nice. And you led me to believe you didn't know anyone in San Diego. You've played this scramble before with Kirsten. I'm assuming that means you know someone in town."

"I just wanted you to take pity on me," he admitted.

"I feel used."

"But hopefully in a good way?" He grinned.

Yes, dammit, in a good way.

"I have a terrible feeling this isn't going to go well."

"Don't worry about it. I promise you'll do fine. It's a scramble."

"I don't even know what that means. That's how clueless I am. I keep picturing scrambled eggs."

"It just means that on every hole, after everyone tees off, you choose the best drive and everyone plays from there. It speeds up the game and gives less experienced players a chance to keep up with more experienced players."

"How can I not worry about it?" she continued to fret. "I barely know a five iron from a pitching wedge. What *is* the difference?"

He laughed. "Patti will help you with that. Do you think Kirsten is that great of a golfer?"

"She's not?"

"She only plays in scrambles because she's not good enough to play any other way."

"Oh, well then, I do feel a little better." Eva grinned. "Does that make me petty?"

"It makes you human."

"Can't argue with that."

"Kirsten is here for the charity and to rub elbows with celebrities. Take a page from her playbook. Have a good time."

"Sports metaphors. How come guys always have to talk in sports metaphors?"

"I think it's genetic. Something in our Y chromosome."

"Apparently."

"Your last boyfriend spoke in sports metaphors?"

"Why do you want to know so much about him? I told you, it's over. Ancient history. Wasn't really anything to begin with."

"Just curious. I want to avoid the same mistakes he made."

"Hang around and you'll do fine. Keith's biggest flaw was that he didn't show up when he said he was going to."

Why had she said that? It sounded desperate. Like she wanted Adam to hang around. Eva notched her chin up. She didn't need anybody.

Adam followed the golf cart in front of them over a quaint little wooden bridge that stretched over a trickling creek. He reached over and took her hand. Held it.

She tried to pull away, but he wouldn't let go.

"It's okay to admit he hurt you," he whispered.

"He didn't. I was just dumb to get involved with him in the first place."

Adam stopped when they reached the green and she hopped from the cart, happy to have her hand back, and dashed for her golf bag before either Adam or Patti could retrieve it. But she couldn't get it unbuckled from the strap on the cart.

Adam came over and pressed his hand against her spine, just above the waistband of her skirt. "Allow me."

She stepped back and let him at it.

"Just friends, huh?" Patti Carson winked as she walked past them to caddy for Kirsten and Teddy.

Teddy teed off first, then Kirsten. Adam went next.

Eva watched him tee up his golf ball, and then take a couple of practice swings. Her gaze fixated on his erect posture, the way his shoulders moved like an orchestrated whole, each part doing its job to drive the little white ball down the long green fairway, his shot surpassing both Kirsten's and Teddy's. He looked so edible. Like homemade brownies or fudge or chocolate chip cookies—something delectable and completely decadent.

And then it was her turn. Up to the tee. Everyone watching.

Ack! She was afraid she was going to miss the ball and spin around in a circle. That's what had happened to her the last time she'd played miniature golf.

She settled the ball on the tee. So far so good. Okay, all right, even if she stunk up the place it was fine. They'd all shoot from where Adam's ball had landed.

"Golfing glove." Patti handed her a pink glove.

"Oh, thank you." She put it on.

"One wood." Patti passed her a club.

"Thanks again," Eva said gratefully, and centered herself over the ball. Now what? This club was really long.

"Step back a little," Adam's voice soothed, his head right beside her ear. "Interlace your fingers like this." He was behind her, his arms, around her, his fingers over hers, guiding her, showing her. "That's it."

His breath was hot on her neck, his back against her spine. Every bone, every nerve, every cell in her body melted.

"Keep your eye on the ball. Never take your eye off the ball," he instructed.

She stared at the ball as if her life depended on it, determined to do him proud.

"Now swing back." With his arms around hers, he pulled back.

They swung in unison. Her gaze riveted to the ball.

"Follow through." He pushed her arms forward in a smooth swinging motion.

Her club hit the ball with a solid *thwack!*

"Keep your eyes on the ball," he murmured.

She tracked it, her arms following her gaze and the ball sailed perfectly straight and true. It didn't go as far as Teddy's or Adam's, but it went smack-dab down the middle of the fairway, rolling far past Kirsten's ball.

"That was beautiful," Adam enthused, wrapping his arms around her waist. He yanked her off her feet and swung her in a circle.

"Put me down," she laughingly demanded. She still had hold of the one wood and she was afraid she was going to accidentally whack someone with it the way he was spinning her around.

Feeling giddy with her success, she giggled and when he settled her back down on the ground his face was so close to hers that she was almost certain he was going to kiss her.

He might have if Kirsten hadn't cleared her throat and said, "Fine, we play Adam's ball."

She strode to her golf cart, Teddy scurrying behind her.

"Somebody's miffed that you showed her up," Adam chuckled softly.

"I was only able to do it because you helped me." Eva grinned.

Another group of golfers was behind them, waiting to tee off, surrounded by cameras and spectators. Eva realized one was a well-known actor and she was struck again by how out of place she was here.

The sun had disappeared behind a bank of clouds smothering out the last remaining fingers of daylight. She'd heard warnings on the radio that morning that the heat was pushing potential thunderstorms up from Mexico. She hadn't paid much attention to it at the time, but now the air felt sluggish and swollen with rain and the wind had picked up, sending little eddies of dirt swirling around the course.

They drove to their balls that sat glowing phosphorous-green on the fairway. They played a few more rounds, using Adam's position to play from almost every time. Once or twice Teddy surpassed him, but never Kirsten or Eva.

And each time she was up to tee, Adam would come up behind her, put his arms around her and walk her through the shot. She loved golf, Eva decided. It was a very misunderstood game.

After the fourth hole, however, the weather that had been pouting and broody turned altogether mean. The wind snarled through the trees, snatching at the canopies of the golf carts and distant lightning lit up the sky. The air smelled of sulfur and thunder rumbled a warning. *Go home, fools.*

In the end, the sponsors called off the game. She and Adam had come in separate cars. They loaded up both sets of golf clubs in his trunk and he insisted on following her home, especially since her Jeep didn't have a top. It didn't start raining until they turned into the covered parking area of the apartment complex. Then the sky let loose.

Laughing, the wind whipping her hair madly about her face, Eva darted from her Jeep just as Adam stepped from his Maxima and opened an umbrella.

"You're always prepared," she said, feeling utterly breathless as he sheltered her from the rain.

"And you never are."

"That's half the adventure," she said. "Never knowing what's around the next corner."

They were standing in the courtyard now, huddled together beneath his umbrella, the lightning moving closer, the thunder growing louder.

"Um…" Eva said, "the evening doesn't have to end."

"I think maybe it does."

"You could come up to my place."

He shook his head. "That's not such a good idea."

"Oh," she said, feeling very disappointed. The way he'd been touching her all night had made her skin so sensitive. "Well, okay then. G'night."

Then before he could see the hurt in her eyes, she turned and sprinted for her apartment.

13

TONIGHT, EVA WASN'T DOING naked yoga. Tonight, she was whirling around her living room like a naked dervish, dancing to some wild music he couldn't hear from across the courtyard. Was it hip-hop? Rock? Pop? Rap? With Eva, who knew?

Adam kept his eyes glued to the telescope. Nothing short of an earthquake could compel him to look away. Her pert breasts—just the perfect size—bounced like independent wheel suspension on a luxury car as she leaped and twirled. The woman was an enthusiastic work of art, and he was dating her.

You're not dating her.

Okay, not technically, but Eva thought they were dating. It felt like they were dating. He wanted to be dating her.

She spun, kicked. The butterfly on her back flashed past. It appeared to flutter as she moved. Flying free.

Butterfly.

It was the perfect symbol for Eva. Beautiful and light, unfettered and sensual.

Why was *she* interested in him? What did he have to offer a woman like her? She could literally have any man she wanted. Who wouldn't be drawn to her joie de vivre? Who wouldn't ache to kiss those lips, to run his palms over her skin, to slip his fingers through her hair? She was the most amazing creature and he couldn't have her. Not for the long run. It was like Kirsten had said. He and Eva fit together like peanut butter and sausage. Still, he couldn't help wishing, hoping.

Yeah, all that will fall apart when she finds out that you're just hanging out with her because of Barksdale.

And he wasn't even doing his job worth a damn. He was supposed to have planted a listening device in her cell phone tonight, but he'd gotten so caught up in teaching her to play golf, he'd completely forgotten about looking for an opportunity to do what he'd been assigned to do.

How he wished things were different. That they could be a real couple, really dating. He wondered when he'd started yearning for her so consistently.

It had come in measures, starting with the pure thrust of lust when he'd first gotten a peek at her doing naked yoga. His desire had grown steadily with each encounter he'd had with her, rooting deeper and deeper the more he got to know her. She was everything he was not and he knew that when this was over he'd forever have an empty feeling because she was no longer part of his life.

She's not part of your life. She's just an assignment.

He could tell himself that all day long, but it wouldn't make it true. He wanted her with a vengeance.

The rain pelted against the window, clouding his view, but he could still see her through the streaks of water, dancing and dancing.

His need was a living thing—growing, burning, yearning. He had to have her.

Lightning flashed, bathing the dark courtyard in a split-second illumination of light. Thunder followed with a window-jarring crack.

He couldn't deny his need any longer. He'd tried his best. Fallen back on every trick he knew. He had to have her. He didn't care what it meant for his career.

That scared the shit out of him, but fear was no longer enough to hold him. The temptation was too great. The spell Eva had cast over him too intoxicating.

On and on she danced.

He could unzip his pants and satisfy himself as best he could, as he'd done on other lonely nights, but he knew it was no longer enough. He craved the feel of her body, the taste of her tongue, the smell of her hair. He was in knots over her and there was no undoing them. He had to have her.

The rain fell in buckets now, drenching the courtyard. He could barely see her. She was just a beautiful blur. But he imagined that her breath was coming in sexy, heavy pants, timed with the throbbing of the song. The tempo seemed to pound out *Eva, Eva, Eva* against the back of his brain.

Compelled, he got up from the stool. He wasn't thinking. All rationality was gone. He only reacted, following the dictates of his body. He rushed out the door.

Instantly, he was drenched in the torrential downpour, his shirt plastered to his chest, his hair plastered to his head. He clambered down the steps, sprinted across the courtyard, the tune in his head driving him, driving him. *Eva, Eva, Eva.*

Up her stairs he went, two at a time. He was breathing hard, not from the exertion——he was in excellent shape——but from anticipation.

Saliva filled his mouth. Hunger tore at him. Eva was the only thing that could sate him. No other woman would do. Not now. Not ever.

Flashdance. She'd been whirling to *Flashdance*. The sound track from the old movie spilled from her apartment.

He reached her door. Lifted a fist. Thumped on it. *Wham, wham, wham*.

"Eva!" He yelled her name like Marlon Brando in *A Streetcar Named Desire*. No, more like William Hurt smashing through a window with a chair to get to Kathleen Turner in *Body Heat*.

He was that driven, that determined to get to her. That out of his mind for her.

She'd reduced him to this. Out of control, crazed, ruled by sex and need. Dammit, he was drowning and loving every minute of it. His career was unraveling and he didn't care. Eva was all that mattered. She was both his salvation and his destruction.

"Eva!"

She yanked open the door. At some point on his mad trek over there, she'd wriggled into yoga pants and a T-shirt, but her feet were still bare, her hair a wild tumble about her shoulders. "Wh—"

He didn't give her a chance to speak. Just reached up with his palms and captured her face between them. He looked her squarely in the eyes and then he kissed her. Kissed her with every ounce of passion that had been growing inside him since the first moment he'd seen her. Kissed her until neither one of them could breathe. The cold wind blew water over them. He was getting her soaking wet.

Apparently, she didn't care. She reached up, wrapped her arms around his neck and pulled him over the threshold. He stood there dripping water on her hardwood floor.

"Eva, I—"

"Shh, shh."

She didn't want to talk. That was fine with him. He'd always been a man of action, anyway. He didn't speak another word, just leaned over to scoop her into his arms and stalked toward her bedroom.

"At last," she said. "I wondered how long I was going to have to get naked in front of that window before you came to get me."

HIS LIPS! SHE'D BEEN WAITING so long to taste his lips.

Adam held her tightly, as if he'd sooner have his arms chopped off than ever let her go.

Lightning flared outside the window. Thunder crashed as loud as if it had been in the same room with them. They both startled as the electricity snapped off, amputating the *Flashdance* beat in midthump and bathing them in black silence. The only sound was their raspy breathing and a distant wail of an ambulance siren.

Her bedroom was completely dark. Oh, this wouldn't do, she needed to see him.

"Hang on," he said, as though reading her thoughts. He set her down. "I'm just going to get some of those candles from the living room."

He returned a second later with two vanilla-scented candles in his hands. He settled them on the top of her bureau, and then turned to draw her into his arms again.

His hot mouth took possession of hers and she felt

herself melting against him as his strong arms pulled her closer. His solid erection pressed hard against her thigh.

Sensation swamped Eva's body. Enveloped her in a snug embrace. Her nose twitched with the earthy smell of him. Her lips tingled, anxious to taste his raw, masculine energy. Goose bumps rippled over her skin at the heat radiating off him. Her fingers splayed over the wet T-shirt clinging to his chest and she felt his thudding heart as she heard her own heartbeat pounding through her eardrums.

Welcomed. She felt welcomed.

He pushed her back against the wall, glaring down at her. "Woman, you can't keep driving me crazy. Naked yoga. Naked dancing."

"So," she murmured in a soft, teasing tone. "You like to watch."

"It's not—"

She laid a finger against his lips, breaking off his words. "Shh, you don't have to lie. I'm not mad."

"You're not?"

Eva leaned into him, felt the heat rolling off his muscular body. "I find the idea sexy."

"You do?" he croaked.

"It's so naughty." She splayed a palm to his chest and pushed him backward until he planted his feet by the end of the bed.

His eyes flashed fire and he growled low in his throat as he lowered his head to nibble at her throat. She realized she could lose herself in this man. Fully, completely—and that scared her more than anything. If she were smart, she'd ask him to leave.

But she couldn't. She didn't want him to leave. She wanted him to make love to her all night long.

"Adam," she whispered.

His body surrounded hers. His eyes had darkened. His hand was tight around her wrist.

Her flesh burned from her heart to her stomach, straight down to her sex. Burned and ached and craved.

His mouth claimed her.

She might not want to admit she belonged to him, but her body had other plans. Involuntarily, she arched against him, her pelvis grinding against his. His erection was granite. No, harder than granite.

"Eva," he rasped.

She opened her mouth to tell him to take her, but his tongue darted between her parted teeth and she got nothing out but a soft sound of exhalation. He swallowed her up in one heady gulp. She didn't even know how it happened but one minute he again had her back pressed up against the wall, the next minute he had his knees shoved between her legs, prying them apart, while he bent his head to suckle her nipple through the cotton material of her T-shirt.

"You like things wild?"

"Yes," she gasped.

"You like it hot and furious?"

"I do."

"Then that's the way I'm going to give it to you. Hot and hard and fast. You're going to take every inch of me and when we're done, then we're going to do it the way I like. Soft and slow and sweet."

Her entire body liquefied at his words. "Oh, Adam."

His hands slipped underneath the hem of her shirt, his mouth still nibbling at her nipple.

She threaded her fingers through his hair, threw her head back against the wall and let out a low moan. He pushed her shirt up around her waist, slid a hot palm down the waistband of her yoga pants. She writhed, twisted against him.

He pushed his index finger into her. He wasn't gentle, but neither was he rough. Just firm and determined, letting her know he was in charge and she was at the whim of his bidding.

It was incredibly erotic. Knowing this man wanted her and knew how to please her. A man she could truly trust. She wriggled against the feel of his finger. She had to have more.

When he slipped the second finger inside her, she moaned again.

He raised his head, ran his other hand through her hair, pinned her to him as his mouth drank from hers again.

His taste intoxicated her. Bowled her over. His tongue was doing crazy things to her. Things she'd never felt before. Things she'd never believe possible. She was helpless to resist. He owned her and it felt glorious.

Adam lightly pinched her nipples with one hand, while the other was still embedded into her. Three fingers now, shoving into her. His chest pushed against her, kept her pressed against the wall. "You like the way my hand feels inside you?"

Mutely, she nodded.

"You haven't felt anything yet," he said. "Just wait until you have my cock buried inside you as far as you can take it."

She groaned.

"That's right, baby. By the time I let you come, you're going to explode."

His hand continued to pump against her, while his thumb, his wicked, wicked thumb, strummed the straining nub at her entrance. Each stroke took her higher and higher on an updraft of sensation until her breathing was nothing more than shallow strings of air, barely eking through the passageway of her lungs.

Nothing had ever felt this intense. His mouth was on hers, then it was gone, nipping at her nipples, then it was back again, leaving her dizzy and delighted.

And all the while his hand worked her over, giving her no rest, no respite.

"Adam, Adam, take me," she begged.

"Not yet. Not by a long shot."

"You're so mean," she ground out through gritted teeth.

"Payback's a bitch," he whispered.

She supposed he was referring to the way she'd been leaving the curtain slightly ajar when she'd done yoga in the nude, hoping that he was watching her. She smiled. But had she been this relentless?

Her body tensed, she was on the verge of coming, his magical hand stoking her higher and hotter…

And then suddenly he just stopped.

"Wh…" It was the only sound she could push through her constricted throat.

He pulled his hand from her panties. She could smell her own scent. Feel her body throbbing. She felt robbed, cheated.

He held her tight against his chest, his heart pounding as fiercely as hers. Amazingly his erection was harder than before.

"Arms up," he instructed.

She couldn't have disobeyed him if she'd wanted to. She raised her hands over her head and he grabbed the hem of her T-shirt and tugged it over her head. At the sight of her bare breasts, a groan slipped from his lips.

"Eva," he murmured. "My sweet Eva."

He was suckling her again. Did he have any idea how much that turned her on? He was a wizard, instinctively knowing just where to touch her and with how much pressure. It was as if he'd been given a map to her body and he'd spent a lifetime studying it.

"Your turn," she said when she couldn't bear the torture anymore and wrestled his wet T-shirt over his head.

She ran her palms over the planes of his chest, but when she tried to hone in on his nipples the way he'd done to her, he put up a hand to block her.

"No," he said. "Tonight is all about you. You touch my nipples and I won't last five minutes."

"Good to know," she said.

"I'm giving away all of my secrets," he said.

"So am I," she whispered. "I'm trusting you not to hurt me."

He looked deeply into her eyes. "I won't betray your trust, Eva."

"You promise?"

"I swear to it."

She wrapped her arms around his neck and pulled his head down in a kiss. His hands were tugging off her yoga pants, pulling them to the floor. She kicked out of them.

He encircled her waist with his hands and twirled her across the room, leaving her clothes behind. She wore nothing now except her panties. He still had on his blue jeans.

She reached for his belt buckle. "Let's get you out of those."

"Oh, no, not yet. C'mere." He took her hand, led her over to the bed. "Sit."

She sat, nerve endings tingling.

He dropped on his knees in front of her.

"Adam...what are you doing...I...don't really like that."

"You don't like oral sex?"

Oral sex had always made her feel slightly ashamed and she didn't know why. Most guys were relieved that she didn't want them to go there.

"It makes me feel...embarrassed."

"There's no reason to feel embarrassed, Sunshine. Not with me."

"I—"

"Shh." He pressed a finger against her lips. "You're the one who's so good at relaxing and letting go. Just lie back and enjoy this."

She started to protest again, but he was kissing her navel and instant tingles spread downward. He was right. She took a deep breath, leaned back and just allowed him to do as he wished.

He spread her legs wide, moving her hips until she was in a froglike position. Lightly, he tickled her inner thighs. The sensation had her squirming against him. She grabbed a couch pillow and pressed it to her lips to keep from groaning as his mouth traveled lower and lower until the tip of his tongue touched her hot clit.

"Sweet," he cooed. "So damned sweet."

She didn't know what to say or how to react, but nature took over. Her hips arched upward of their own volition, seeking his mouth.

He chuckled low and deep. "That's my girl."

Eva luxuriated in the moment, in awe that she was here in bed with this man—a man who had the potential to change her entire life. She'd never been one to give a man that much power, but with Adam, she just wanted to let go. He made her believe that anything was possible.

He dipped his head down to her sex, but stopped just short of touching her with his tongue. His breath was hot against her tender flesh, igniting her.

Eva arched her hips, trying to bring his mouth and her clit into contact, but he read her like a map and moved with her, keeping his mouth just out of her reach.

"Beast," she hissed.

He chuckled.

"You've got a cold heart."

"Hang on, Sunshine. We'll get there."

She liked the way he called her *Sunshine*. A warm endearment. But she didn't want to hang on. She wanted him to make love to her with his mouth *right now*. Her brain was glazed with lust, her body worked to a fevered pitch.

Gently he spread her thighs wider and moved his body around so that he could kneel between her legs. "You are so beautiful."

The head of his penis throbbed against her inner thigh as he leaned forward. Eva's excitement escalated. She couldn't stand this. She'd never felt such desperate pressure.

His big fingers caressed her gently as his tongue explored her silky folds. Her eyes slid closed, savoring what he was doing.

"Yes," she whispered. "Yes."

His teeth tenderly captured her clit.

Never, in all her life, had she experienced this kind of pleasure. It was ecstasy. He seemed to know exactly what she wanted, what she needed from him. Knew it even better than she did. He reveled in her and she had never felt so cherished. It was dangerous territory, these sweet feelings. But she couldn't stop them. They were part and parcel of what was going on.

All her senses were altered—sound, sight, taste, smell, touch. She existed in an uncharted but delicious land. Total awareness. Barbed strands of fevered sensation pricked her throbbing sex. Her inner muscles contracted, wanting him.

"You are the hottest woman in the world," he breathed.

She scaled the mountain of arousal, pushed upward by his tongue. She hovered on the brink of orgasm but he would not let her fall over. A steady strumming vibration began deep in her throat and it emerged as a wild moan.

"Please," she begged. "Please."

"Ask me," he whispered.

"Please, please, please make me come."

He gave her everything then, his tongue, his fingers, his lips. She let go and just allowed him to take her over. He seemed to be everywhere—over her, around her, inside of her, outside of her. He was unbelievable.

"Almost," she gasped. "Almost there."

It washed over her in a sudden wave, big and full. She rode the crest, surfing it to the shore.

And when the wave had trickled away, he pulled her into the crook of his arm and held her tightly for a very long time.

14

"I NEVER IMAGINED YOU could be such a bad boy," Eva said some time later, and moved from his arms to straddle him.

"And that turns you on?" Adam reached up and spanned her waist with both hands, trapping her between his thighs. Disappointment warred with his desire for her. Of course she liked bad boys. She'd been with Barksdale, hadn't she?

Well, you're not exactly a choirboy, Mancuso. You're breaking all the rules here.

Yeah and he wasn't one bit proud of himself, but dammit there were just some things beyond a man's control. An overpowering urge to join his body with Eva St. George was one of them.

She loomed over him, confident in her sexuality, her eyes glistening in the muted candlelight, fully accustomed to getting what she wanted.

She leaned down to rest her forehead against his, and peered into his eyes. "Do you watch me every night?"

He licked his lips and spoke the truth. "Yes."

"Do you touch yourself when you watch me?"

"Umm, sometimes," he admitted.

She moved, hooking her legs around his. Her bottom pressed against his thighs. She might look cool and in control, but he felt her tremble. Knew she was as excited as he.

Her fingers lightly tickled his abdomen. "Do you come when you watch me?"

He'd been assigned to watch her, but it had gone far beyond the job. As he'd watched he'd fantasized about a moment just like this one, but in all honesty, he'd never really dreamed it could happen. A naked Eva straddling his body, the sweet smell of her invading his nostrils, turning his mind into a pile of mush.

His hands traveled from her waist to her shoulders. Her lean arms were simultaneously muscular yet soft, a delightful contrast.

Eva herself was a compilation of contrasts. At once disciplined enough to run her own business, but free-flowing enough for surfing. She was unfettered and yet at the same time one of the most grounded women he'd ever known. She was comfortable in her own skin and yet at the oddest moments a vulnerability would settle over her as it had at the golf scramble with Kirsten and Teddy.

She was childlike and yet mature, sharp-tongued and gentle, soft and firm. She was his dream and his demon.

And hot.

So damned hot.

He shouldn't want her, but he did. He shouldn't *need* her—but he did.

She tossed her hair and he felt it like a punch to his gut. Everything she did, every move she made affected him on a visceral level. Her smile got him hard.

Her touch gave him goose bumps. Her laugh made his knees weak.

She made him feel…well, that was just it, wasn't it? She made him feel.

Adam hadn't realized how long he'd been emotionally numb. Blunted by the demands of his job and his desire to succeed. Whether he was irritated or delighted, worried or turned-on, whenever he was around Eva he felt those emotions he'd kept smothered for so long.

His skin tingled and he was acutely aware of everything. The way the candlelight threw shadows across her face, and illuminated her in a soft glow. Angels couldn't look this pretty, tousled and tossed. He smiled, remembering how responsive she'd been when he pressed his mouth to her most intimate part.

She'd turned him inside out and upside down. She'd opened the floodgates of emotions and everything had come pouring out. This woman who some might see as little more than ordinary, was the most extraordinary thing that had ever happened to him. He saw now what Kirsten had meant when she'd broken up with him. He felt as if he'd been sleepwalking through life until this moment—until Eva.

Why hadn't anyone warned him he could feel this way? He hadn't thought to protect against it, because until now, he'd never felt it—this kind of love.

Every thought that rose in his mind was "we" or "us." He couldn't picture his life without her and that was alarming, mostly because he'd been lying to her. Yes, it was part of his job, but he hated it. He had to tell her the truth, even if it meant violating a direct order from his commander.

She was like a daisy, all bright and hearty, but that was on the outside. On the inside, he knew she'd been hurt, kept those hurts buried, but felt them nonetheless. She didn't want anyone to see her vulnerabilities so she kept things light, pretended she didn't care. But he knew she cared. It was in the way she looked at him, the way she touched him, the way she opened her heart up to him even though she knew she might get hurt again. And here he was with the ability to crush that heart.

Dammit. Why had this happened? Why had he met her under these circumstances? Why couldn't they have met in an ordinary way?

She thinks you did meet in an ordinary way. She thinks you're just her neighbor.

"Why are you staring at me like that?" she asked.

A lump formed in his throat. He had to tell her the truth. But how to start? "Sunshine."

"Is that your nickname for me? Are you being sappy, Adam Mancuso?"

"I suppose I am." He smiled.

"And here I thought you weren't the sappy type."

"You make me sappy."

"Don't try to blame this on me." She laughed, her blond hair tumbling about her shoulders in wild disarray. "You're sappy to the core."

"I'm not."

"You call me Sunshine."

"Because you have such a sunny disposition."

"That's sappy."

"And you love it."

She grinned. "Sap."

"Sunshine."

"I remember you promised me hard, hot sex."

"Ah," he said. "I suppose I did."

"C'mon. Let's take a shower."

"Together?"

She reached for his hand. "Yes, together. What? You've never showered with a woman before?"

Honestly, no. But that wasn't why he hesitated. He was thinking about how to break the news.

"Let's go." She tugged on his arm.

"Showering together? And you're calling me a sap."

"Showering together isn't sappy, it's sexy. There's a big difference."

"You're going to have to illustrate the point for me because I'm not seeing the difference."

"Oh, have no fear. Eva's here." She giggled and drew him off the bed, her bare little rump dancing as she yanked on his arm.

He followed. He loved to go where she led. She took him to places he'd never been before. She stretched him in ways he'd never considered. Stretched him so much in fact, he feared he could never return to the shape and form he'd been before. How did you go back to your old mindset once your eyes had been opened?

Once they were in the darkened bathroom, she pulled matches from a drawer and lit a plethora of candles scattered around the bathroom. The woman certainly knew how to set a scene.

She danced him over to the shower, opened the clear glass door and stepped inside, taking him with her. Impishly, she kissed his arm as she simultaneously reached around to turn on the shower. She jumped and squealed as the cold water hit their skin and he maneuvered past her to turn up the heat. The water temperature evened out.

"Eva—" He started to tell her that there was something they needed to talk about after their shower was over. Something he needed to tell her before things went any further. But her arms were around his neck and she was pulling his head down for a kiss and he was a goner.

His dick took his brain hostage.

He kissed her back, fiercely. Mine, he thought. My woman.

Usually he was not the possessive type, but with Eva—well, with Eva there was no usually. Everything was different with her and he loved it.

She moved her lips from his mouth and nibbled down the length of his chin to his throat.

Adam braced himself with both arms against either wall of the shower as she slipped lower and lower and lower....

Her mouth touched the head of his penis as water splashed against his chest. His mind whirled. He wanted to tell her to stop, because what she was doing was making a muddle of his head, but what she was doing felt too good, too fine.

He held his breath and then let it out in a long hiss of air as she worked him over with that hot tongue of hers. Glory. Pure glory.

How come he'd never showered with a woman before? It was incredible. She was incredible.

"Eva." He groaned.

While her mouth was occupied with his penis, her hands drifted around to cup his buttocks. Her fingers sank into his flesh, kneading his muscles.

The pleasure! Such *unbelievable* pleasure.

He felt her everywhere. On his skin, in his heart, inside his brain. Her frisky tongue flicked him in ways he'd never been flicked. She was a goddess, his Eva.

His Eva.

He had to shake that thought. She couldn't be his.

Not yet. Maybe not ever. Once she learned he'd been betraying her...

"Eva," he murmured, and reached for her, trying to break her from what she was doing so that they could talk. They had to have this talk.

But she mistook his actions and quickened her pace. Increasing suction, doing more wild things to him. His mind went blank. He could not think. Could not do anything except submit. Whatever she wanted, he would give to her. Sun, moon, stars, it didn't matter. He would get it for her, whatever she wanted.

He felt the rumbling of his orgasm surge up through his shaft and just when he thought it was a foregone conclusion, she stopped.

"Argh!" The strangled cry shot from his throat as a sharp ache tightened around his cock.

"Now," she said. "I want you inside me."

"Wha...?" His mind was gone; a complete sieve.

He wasn't even thinking of condoms, but she reached outside the shower and suddenly she had one and then she was rolling it on him with her tongue. When she was done, she got to her feet.

Adam pulled her to him and kissed her so hard and long she was gasping. Then he grabbed her around the waist and turned her toward the wall. "Brace yourself," he said.

She leaned forward, both palms placed against the wall under the showerhead, her gorgeous butt even with his cock. She twitched her fanny, tempting him, bewitching him. "Come and get me."

He didn't stand a chance. The sight of her sexy back stretching out underneath the water spray was his utter undoing.

Droplets rolled down the small of her back and came

to rest on her rump, bathing her in a glistening light. He tightened his grip on her waist with both hands. She was slick and wet and he was mindless. He plunged in, crazed as crazy could be. Pushed himself in to the hilt.

"So good," she moaned. "Adam, it feels so good to have you up inside me this way. Give it to me. Make me scream."

He let loose, pumping and pounding against her lush backside, her sweet ass.

She reached between her legs to find and cup his balls and he lost all the air in his lungs.

"Harder, harder," she begged.

If that's what she wanted, then that's what he would give her. His goddess. He slammed into her with more force than he thought possible, lifting her up with each thrust.

"Don't stop, don't stop," she chanted. "Adam, Adam, Adam."

"Tell me what you want." He kept driving into her. "Is this what you want?"

"More, more…" came her hoarse gasp.

He was terrified he was going to disappoint her. That he was going to come before she got her orgasm. He was too close. If he kept on this way he was going to lose it. He had to do something to hurry up her orgasm.

Still holding on to her with one hand, he slipped his other hand down and eased his fingers over her mound until he found what he was looking for.

The minute he touched her clit he felt her inner muscles tighten around his cock, heard her rugged intake of air. "Yeah, baby, you like that?"

She couldn't answer, only moaned and nodded.

"That's right." He kept thrusting, pushing hard while

his finger massaged her swollen little nub. "That's right."

He'd never done this with anyone. Been so aggressive while at the same time so tender. She brought out the beast in him, but she was the lion tamer, cracking her whip.

She opened up new worlds for him. When he was with her, his neurons fired differently, making new pathways in his brain. She was uncharted territory, pushing him to the limits of his endurance.

Eva said a very naughty word that lit him up inside.

Adam didn't need any more urging than that. He was on it. Giving her what she begged him for. Utter release. He let go of everything—his thoughts, his fears, his embarrassment.

Adam Mancuso let down his guard. Let her in. Her body consumed his, pulling him in deeper and deeper and deeper until he knew there was no getting out of this. He was in this up to the hilt and he didn't want to be anywhere else on the planet. He was inside Eva St. George and there wasn't anything that felt better.

Her hot, slick hands were still on his balls, tugging gently, causing them to pull up tight against his body. His hand was still on her clit, strumming purposefully. He was buried inside of her, grunting and grappling and feeling every inch of her. Knowing that this was the place he belonged forever and always. Eva.

"Adam," she whimpered.

It happened then.

In a crack of a second.

Both of them breaking together like ocean waves. He was a surfer and she was the tunnel. He was in her and she was around him and they were one, riding together in a glorious, indescribable shoot-out. His cock jerked.

Her body collapsed against his. They were panting and soaking wet.

He tightened his grip around her waist and slowly, they sank down to the bottom of the shower, the water—gone cold now—beating softly against their heated skin.

15

EVA WOKE UP AFTER THE BEST SEX of her life in a total panic. Following their escapade in the shower, they'd made love again. This time in the soft bed, slow and gentle and for a very long time, just as Adam had promised.

She'd finally found a man who kept his promises. Eva sighed as her chest tightened. *Be careful.*

Adam lay on his stomach in her bed, his arms thrown across her waist, his face buried in the pillow. Just looking at him made her heart skip erratically.

What in the hell have you done?

She'd sworn to herself that she was not going to sleep with him this soon. That this time she was going to take things slow, not jump headlong into a relationship with a man she did not really know and poof! Look what she'd done.

This was a disaster.

She lay in the weak light of dawn, staring at the ceiling, her body achy in all the right places, her brain working overtime trying to find a way out of this. God, did she not possess one ounce of self-control? When he'd shown up on her doorstep, soaked to the skin, looking wild and ravenous, her knees had almost buckled.

And when he'd clamped his palms around her face and kissed her like it was the end of the world, hell, she'd been noodle soup. Who could have resisted such a fierce seduction from such a quiet man? She'd reduced him to beastly behavior and she'd thrilled in her power.

That fact was disturbing in and of itself. Never mind that she was having all kinds of feelings she couldn't define. This was scary stuff and she had to find a way out of it.

A coyote would gnaw its leg off.

What are you so afraid of? A clear voice in the back of her mind asked the question, but she had no rational answer. Honestly, she was scared he could be The One. That this could be right. That he, that she...

She was afraid to express what she really wanted. She was afraid to hope.

So many times in her life she'd gotten her hopes up, only to have them dashed. She'd loved that town in New Mexico, where her mother had moved in with a guy who'd driven a purple hearse.

She'd made friends. They'd lived in a bungalow at the base of a mountain. She'd planned on learning to ski. Then before the first good snow, her mother had said she had restless feet. The guy who drove the hearse was too clingy. She needed air or she couldn't breathe. She'd bought a ragtag car from a used car lot, stuck Eva in the backseat and taken off at five o'clock in the morning before the hearse guy woke up.

Running again. From what or why Eva never knew. But she remembered the wretched disappointment of leaving behind a place she'd started to love. Yet again.

Somewhere along the way, she'd stopped hoping.

Sure, she'd grown up, forgiven her mother, let go of the past. But part of it was still with her. The part where she was always waiting for the other shoe to drop. The part of her that never really believed in anything permanent, because nothing was permanent so you'd best live in the moment, live *for* the moment. Which was what she'd done last night.

And now...

She was left with the consequences. A man in her bed. A man she wanted to keep forever. A man she knew nothing about.

Shit, Eva, you did it again.

Guilt stole over her. Why couldn't she control herself? Why was she so impulsive? Why did she have to feel so intensely?

The big question was what was she going to do about Adam? In her experience, it was only after you slept with them that guys got truly invested in you. They started expecting things. Things she didn't have the power to give. Not now. Not yet. Adam was too soon. He was too much man for her.

There it was. The real reason. In the past she'd been more likely to hook up with man-boys, the kind of guys who hadn't grown up yet. Some of them never would. Guys who offered her nothing more than a good time. Or exciting bad boys like Keith who'd made her blood rev. But she'd never been with a serious guy. A responsible man who honored his commitments. If after sleeping with her, Adam felt committed to her, well...that was a problem because she certainly wasn't ready to commit to him.

Okay, she knew she was waffling. And panicking. Yes, she was panicking. She kept thinking about coyotes and paw-gnawing. She had to make sure he understood that this was a one-time thing. That while it had been fun it really shouldn't happen again. That she really couldn't be in love with him because she'd only known him, what? Ten days?

Why is that? asked the clear voice she kept trying to bury. *Why are you trying to break things off with the first good man you've ever been with?*

Fine. All right. She'd admit it. She was into self-sabotage as surely as her mother had been. But Mom had met Mike and everything had turned around for them. They'd gotten settled. Finally had a home. Could Adam be her Mike?

What precisely was she running from? Why wasn't the fact that Adam was in her bed a good thing?

"Eva?"

Oh, hell, he was awake and she hadn't gotten anything sorted out.

"You awake?" he asked.

She could pretend to be asleep and hope he would leave, but he tightened his grip around her waist and pulled her closer as he turned over.

"Uh-huh," she said.

"Morning," he murmured, and kissed the tip of her nose.

"Hey!" she protested. "You have minty breath. When did you get up to brush your teeth?"

He had the good manners to look guilty. "A few minutes ago while you were still sleeping. You had a new toothbrush in your bathroom drawer. Is it okay that I used it?"

"No fair. You've got a distinct advantage over me."

"I couldn't risk you kicking me out of bed over morning breath."

"What's going to keep you from kicking me out of bed over morning breath?"

"For one thing, it's your bed," he said, angling his mouth down to hers. "For another, you don't have morning breath."

"You are such a liar, but keep it up."

"Last night was—you were—well, *amazing* doesn't begin to cover it."

"Right back at you, big guy."

He nuzzled close to her, kissed her neck. "You drive me insane, woman. And usually I've got a pretty good grip on my self-control. But you...but you...wow."

Wow, indeed.

"Um..." she said. "I think it might be a good idea if we had a talk."

"Okay." His tongue was doing crazy things to her.

She pushed her head down, trying to wriggle away. "Before we get involved in any more of that, we need to have a talk."

He pulled back. "Is something wrong?"

"Not wrong, um...not really. I just wanted to clear the air, get something straight."

"Okay." He propped himself up against the headboard, crossing his arms over his chest. That incredible chest that made her want to bite her lip it was so yummy. "Let's talk."

"I really enjoyed last night," she said. "Don't think I didn't enjoy it. The sex was great, the best. I came like a Fourth of July rocket."

He smiled. God, he was so gorgeous when he smiled. She wished he would stop smiling. "Me, too."

She moistened her lips. He looked so earnest. She wanted to tell him that this was a one-time thing, but she just couldn't make her mouth form the words. Instead, she looked into his eyes and said, "Are you a breakfast eater?"

WHILE EVA BUSTLED AROUND her kitchen whipping up breakfast—he'd offered to help but she'd said the space was too small and shooed him out—Adam came back down to reality.

Last night had been the most amazing night of his life and it was all because of Eva. But, in the process, he'd forgotten who he was and what he'd been sent to do. Higgins was still expecting him to tap her cell phone.

Her purse hung from the doorknob in the hallway. It was unzipped and he could see her cell tucked into the corner. This was his chance to do his job.

"Coffee?" Eva called from the kitchen.

"Yep."

"I'll brew some up. I'm more of a smoothie girl, myself, but I keep coffee in the house for when my friends come over."

"Sounds good." He pulled the listening device from the pocket of his jeans and slunk toward her purse. He felt like a petty thief betraying her trust like this, and almost pivoted on his heel, marched into the kitchen and told her everything.

But what if she was involved with Barksdale?

He didn't believe it. Not in his heart. But the ONI had trained his head. He felt torn in two pieces. How could his allegiances be so equal? On the one hand was his career and his country. On the other was a woman he'd known just a little over a week. How was it possible that her opinion of him meant as much as his job?

Before he could back out, he plunged his hand into

her purse and retrieved the cell phone. He darted a quick glance over his shoulder to make sure she wasn't standing behind him, then dismantled the phone, inserted the listening device and put it back together within a couple of furtive minutes. Basic Cell Phone Bugging 101. Get in, get out, get it done.

"Breakfast is ready."

He slipped the cell phone back into her purse and straightened.

"What were you doing?" she asked, going up on tiptoes to kiss his cheek when he wandered into the kitchen.

"Looking for a pen and paper so I could write down your phone number."

"Oh."

"You were going to give me your number weren't you?"

"Yeah," she said, but her voice went up in pitch. "Sure." She leaned over and plucked a business card from beneath a magnet anchoring it to the refrigerator. "Here. All my contact numbers are on my card."

He slipped the card into his back pocket. "Thanks."

"How do you take your coffee?"

"Hot and black."

She poured the coffee, passed him the cup and then slid two plates of food onto the bistro table in the small dining nook.

Adam took a seat across from her and looked down at his food. "What is this?"

"Waffles and peanut butter with sausage. You've never had it?"

"No."

"It's delicious. It's my favorite breakfast."

There it was, the very thing that Kirsten said didn't

mix. Peanut butter spread over a waffle and topped with sliced sausage patties, maple syrup on the side.

He laughed.

"What's so funny?"

"You never know what strange combination is going to be just perfect together," he said, and then ate the best darned breakfast he'd ever tasted.

AFTER HELPING EVA WITH the dishes, Adam went back to his apartment to set up the receiver to intercept her cell phone calls.

He was sitting on the stool in front of the telescope, staring at her place and thinking about just how spectacular last night had been when the listening device snapped on and he was connected to Eva's outgoing cell phone call.

Rousing himself, he tensed, listened.

"Zoey, I've done it again."

Adam grabbed Eva's dossier, flipped to the section on contacts, and found the name Zoey Sharp. She was Eva's best friend. Now here was proof why he shouldn't be feeling the things he was feeling for Eva. He didn't even know her best friend's name. How could he be falling in love with a woman when he didn't even know her best friend's name?

"Done what?" Zoey asked.

"Hopped into bed too quickly with a guy."

"Eva! I thought you had a moratorium on sex."

"Zoey, this is different. I can't describe it. Adam is the most stable, kind, understanding man that I have ever met. Not to mention he's so good-looking and the best lover I've ever had."

Adam's chest puffed out with pride at that comment.

So he wasn't the only one who'd thought the sex had been super special.

She went on for several minutes, telling her friend about the rained out golf scramble, and how he'd come to her apartment in the middle of the night.

"Sounds like a wild time," Zoey said.

"There's just one thing that worries me."

"What's that?"

"He's got money."

"You mean he's rich?"

"Yes."

"Well, what's wrong with that?"

"I don't fit into that world. The country club was a real eye-opener. That's just not my lifestyle. Can you see me fitting in a place like that?"

"You could if you wanted to."

"I could do it for him. If that's what he wanted."

No, no, no, Adam thought. He loved Eva because she was so certain about who she was. She didn't put on airs. She didn't pull punches. She wasn't a phony. She didn't use people. He loved all those things about her.

"And, Zoey, I trust him. Really trust him. He's not like any of the others."

"Oh, honey, I do so hope you're right. You deserve to have a great guy for once."

"I do, don't I?" Eva laughed. Sunshine. She was always filled with sunshine.

Guilt pushed out the pride and Adam was left knowing he was going to hurt her, disappoint her, betray her trust.

He knew then that he had to tell who he was. What he'd done. Then he would beg and plead for her understanding. He wasn't going to tell Commander Higgins his plan. He'd already learned it was easier to get forgiveness than permission. His gut was telling him what he had to do and he was going to follow it. Orders or no orders.

After Eva ended her phone call with her friend, Adam got out his cell phone and texted her. *Dinner2nite?* Then he wrote in the name of the nicest restaurant on this side of town.

A minute later, she texted back. *Luv2.*

16

THE MAÎTRE D' AT MAISON d'Océan showed them to a romantic table on the back deck overlooking the ocean. White twinkle lights lit up the palm trees and a gentle breeze had Eva pulling her silk wrap up on her shoulders.

After she'd looked up the restaurant on Google and saw how exclusive and expensive it was, she'd gone through her closet in search of something chic enough for the place. She'd come up with a blue silk dress and matching pashmina she'd worn to a wedding a few years back and added a pair of strappy matching sandals. In the jewelry department, the only expensive piece she owned was the platinum locket that Keith had given her. She'd called her hairdresser for an emergency appointment and she'd even splurged on a facial and manicure. Between the golfing outfit and her pampering, she was definitely eating ramen noodles for the rest of the summer.

But damn if it wasn't worth it.

Adam held out her chair for her and she sat, smiling inwardly to herself. The man was chivalrous. She had to give him that.

He settled in across from her. His lips were angular and firm, very masculine. He caught her stare and one corner of his mouth lifted up in a surprisingly rakish grin that changed his face from determined hard-ass to charming rebel without a care. She caught her breath. What had caused the shift? Was it her?

She noticed his gaze tracked the locket that lay nestled perfectly in the V of her cleavage. A smile lit his eyes.

"Pretty locket," he said.

"Thanks." She reached up to finger it. The locket *was* gorgeous and she wasn't about to tell him that another man had given it to her.

"It looks beautiful on you. You're beautiful," he said.

"I'm not, but it's nice to hear you say it."

"You are freaking gorgeous. The way you move…" He hissed in a breath as if he had just been burned.

"You are the best-looking man I've ever dated," she confessed. "Not that we're dating or anything."

"Aren't we?" He let go of the napkin, reached across the table and laid his hand over hers.

His touch was electric. A red-hot jolt that stole her breath and caused a crazy montage of images to flash through her head. She saw them as they must have looked last night, naked in her bed, rolling across the sheets, having a fine old time.

"Are we?"

They stared at each other.

"We're eating out together, talking. Isn't that what people do when they date?"

"I should shut up."

"Don't shut up."

"Why? The more I tell you, the more you're getting pulled into my life."

"So?"

"You don't mind getting pulled into my drama?" She felt a heated glow of emotion light her from the inside out. He made her feel so much, so many different things. Hope and joy, fear and concern.

"Whenever I think about you, I smile. I don't smile a lot, Eva."

"I noticed."

"You make me smile."

"You make me smile, too."

"We better stop smiling or everyone in here is going to think we took Ecstasy or something."

"What I'm feeling has nothing to do with drugs and everything to do with you."

"Adam…" She ducked her head, feeling suddenly inexplicably shy.

"Eva," he whispered. "Look at me."

She lifted her chin.

Adam snagged her gaze, stared deeply into her eyes. He should tell her the truth now, but she looked so pretty and they were having a nice time and they hadn't even ordered their meal yet. She'd gotten dressed up, taken care with her appearance and he was going to ruin everything.

"Yes?"

He ran his hands over her knuckles. "There's something I need to—"

"Would you like to hear about our specials of the day?" asked the chirpy waiter who'd appeared at their table.

The waiter rattled off the items, but Adam didn't hear

a word of it. He kept looking at Eva, thinking how he was about to wreck everything.

"I'll have the red snapper," Eva said when the waiter had finished his spiel.

"And you, sir?"

"That sounds good."

"Can we get wine with that?" Eva asked. "I'd love a glass of wine."

"Bring a bottle," Adam said. He wasn't much of a drinker, but maybe a glass of wine or two would help him find the words he needed to say. *I think I'm falling for you, and oh, by the way, I've been spying on you for the ONI.* "Of your best Chardonnay."

The waiter nodded and departed, leaving them alone in the darkened corner, the soothing sound of the ocean rolling over the shore, the moonlight reflecting off the water.

"This is so romantic," she breathed. "Too romantic."

"What? You don't deserve a little romance?"

"This isn't a little romance, Adam. This is the grand seduction."

"And you don't deserve that, either?"

"I do deserve it," she said, straightening her spine. "But I deserve it with strings attached. I never asked for that before, probably because I never wanted those strings before, but that's what I want now, at this point in my life. Is that going to be a problem, Adam? You can tell me the truth and it will be okay."

Will it? Will it really?

"Because if having strings attached is going to be an issue, we need to stop this thing before one or both of us get hurts."

Too late, he thought. Too late.

"I want someone to do the crossword puzzle with on Sunday mornings and someone who'll make me chicken soup when I have a cold. I want someone I can tell my darkest fears to in the middle of the night and someone to surf with and who'll do yoga with me. Someone whose interests I can share and who'll go with me to my parents' house on the holidays."

I want all those things, too. "After dinner," he said, "let's take a walk on the beach and talk about this."

"Okay," she whispered, her eyes shining with hope. "All right."

Their meal came and they made small talk. He would have thoroughly enjoyed it if his mind hadn't been toying with the scenario ahead of them, worrying how this was all going to play out. Would he lose her just as he'd found her?

He paid the check, then helped Eva from her chair. He drew her close to him and escorted her down off the wooden deck to the beach below.

She leaned into his side and he wrapped his arm across her shoulder, savoring the tender connection he feared would soon be severed.

The locket at her neck glittered in the moonlight while the lanterns from the restaurant above cast shadows over the pylons underneath. It was a perfect spot to steal a stealthy kiss.

The same thought must have crossed her mind, because she stopped, reaching up to wrap her hands around his neck. Adam lowered his head, his mouth already watering to taste her.

Then one of the shadowy pylons moved. Came at them, a blur in the darkness.

Before Adam could react, a form barreled into him, knocking Adam to the ground, and grabbed for the locket around Eva's neck. It took a second for him to realize they were being mugged and it was too dark for him to see the attacker's face clearly.

Eva screamed and clutched her hands around the guy's wrist, while Adam stuck out his leg and tripped him.

The attacker fell in the sand beside Adam, his face turned away.

"Run!" he shouted to Eva.

But his brave woman did not run. She reached down to pick up a piece of driftwood and started smacking the guy in the back of the head.

The guy raised an arm to shield himself against Eva's blows, then the soft driftwood shattered in her hands. The guy leaped up at the same time Adam did and he shoved Eva backward into the water.

"Ooh!" Eva gasped.

The assailant sprinted away as Adam turned to help Eva to her feet. He hadn't been able to catch a clear glimpse of the man's features.

"Run, coward, run!" she yelled as his pounding footsteps echoed into the night.

It was only then that Adam realized she was shaking all over. "Sunshine," he murmured, pulling her to him, not caring that she was wet. "Are you all right?"

"I'm fine, I'm fine, but this dress is silk."

"It's okay. It's just clothing."

"Well, ha! He didn't get my necklace, the slimy thief. This is why I don't wear expensive jewelry. How do you rich people deal with this?"

He had to laugh. "We wear good quality fakes unless we're around security. Do you want to call the cops?"

"No point in that. I couldn't even describe him—could you?"

Adam shook his head.

"He didn't get anything and we'd just be tied up at the police station all night. Take me home instead."

When they got back to their apartment complex, Eva stopped in the courtyard. "I've got an early yoga class in the morning, maybe it's best if we say good night here."

"You're not going to invite me in?"

She shook her head. "We both know what will happen if you come up with me. Neither one of us would get any sleep."

"Are you sure you're all right?" he asked.

"I'm fine," she reassured him. "We'll talk tomorrow."

He kissed her good-night in the courtyard, then watched her walk up to her apartment with longing in his heart. But it was only after his door closed behind him that Adam remembered he'd never told her his secret.

WHEN EVA GOT HOME FROM teaching her yoga class the following morning she was disappointed to see Adam's car was not in his parking space. She'd grown accustomed to him always being around. She'd planned on asking him to have lunch with her at the sandwich shop across the street to apologize for not inviting him up last night. The truth was, things had been moving too fast for her and after they'd been accosted underneath the restaurant, she'd just felt the need to withdraw. She hoped he would understand.

Disappointed, she went on up to her apartment and decided to pop a Lean Cuisine into the microwave for lunch instead.

She'd just pierced the plastic cover of her frozen

dinner with a fork when her cell phone beeped, letting her know she had a text message.

Meet me at the beach just after sunset, pier 16 and wear that locket that makes your cleavage look so tempting. I have a big surprise.

The message had been sent from Adam's iPhone. Eva grinned. Another date. He wasn't mad at her for blowing him off last night. Euphoria ran through her. This time, maybe just maybe, she'd found what she hadn't even known she'd been searching for.

"SOMETHING'S ABOUT TO HAPPEN," Commander Higgins told Adam. "Kilgore and Rogers verified that Barksdale's contact has booked a one-way ticket back to his country of origin. He's leaving tomorrow afternoon. Either Barksdale has already made the deal, or something's happened to him. Either way, I want you off Miss St. George and with Kilgore and Rogers on the buyer."

"We're closing up shop?" Adam asked, stunned.

"I've already sent in the cleaners to remove the surveillance equipment from the apartment."

"Just like that? It's over?"

"No, it's not over at all. You'll be apprehending the contact at the airport."

"I mean with Miss St. George."

"We've been monitoring her phone calls and there's nothing of consequence. Barksdale hasn't approached her again since that day in the ocean. Clearly, she's a dead end."

"That might not be true, sir."

"What do you mean?"

He told his commanding officer about the man who'd attacked them under the pier the previous evening.

"Sounds like a simple mugging to me, Mancuso. You're grasping at straws."

"I think it's a mistake to pull the surveillance off her."

The commander gave him a dark look that told Adam he wasn't a fool. He knew what had been going on between Adam and Eva. "The detail is over, Lieutenant. Report to Kilgore immediately."

17

THE GATHERING DARKNESS had Eva pulling her blouse more tightly around her. After what had happened on the beach last night, she was feeling a bit apprehensive and wondered why Adam had asked her to meet him here.

Part of her wanted to just turn around and head back to her Jeep, call Adam and tell him to meet her in the parking lot. But her adventuresome side, the part of her that liked surprises, forged on.

Nervously, she fingered the locket at her throat. The surprise better be a damned good one.

Maybe, whispered an excited voice in the back of her mind, he's going to tell you that he loves you.

Don't get ahead of yourself. It's much too soon for thoughts like that.

It might be too soon for thoughts like that, but she couldn't help feeling it. Whether she liked it or not, she'd fallen head over heels for Adam Mancuso. For the first time in her life, Eva St. George was in love and she fully realized what she'd been missing.

She felt it to the very depths of her soul, like a solid vibration, like a humming mantra echoing through her every cell.

Adam.

During the day the beach was thronged with families and surfers, everyone out for a good time. But at night things changed. People staggered on the sand, laughing too loud, drinking too much. In the wrong spots, the atmosphere grew more ominous.

The beach in moonlight could be romantic, but a damp mist was rolling in, decreasing visibility, and adding to the brooding mood. Anyone could be out here with nefarious thoughts on their minds.

She wasn't a woman who scared easily. She was tough and resilient and confident in her ability to talk her way out of most predicaments, but tonight, she was spooked. Something just didn't feel right.

A couple of times she thought she felt as if she were being followed. She cast a few glances over her shoulder, but saw no one out of the ordinary.

The most difficult part was walking down the stairway that led to the lower pier. After last night's incident, she was leery. It smelled underneath here, too. Like dead fish and the ripe stench of urine.

She was still several yards from the rendezvous spot where Adam had said to meet him. The people on the beach behind her sounded very far away. It was almost as if she were on another planet. Isolated and alone.

A strong sense of dread washed over her and she fumbled for her phone. No reason to be afraid, she'd just call him, ask him to come to her, even if it ruined his surprise.

She stopped walking to dig in the pocket of her sundress for her cell phone. The hairs on her neck lifted.

Turn, go, run, urged a warning voice in the back of her head.

But she didn't want to give in to panic. That wasn't

the smart thing to do. Neither was coming down here alone. Why would Adam ask her to do it?

She took a deep breath, wishing she'd thought to bring a flashlight. The clouds had moved, obscuring the moon, bathing the beach in almost total darkness. She started to punch in Adam's number, but before she could do so, a hand wrapped around her mouth, while another hand snaked around her waist and pulled her away toward the water.

ADAM DIDN'T CARE THAT Commander Higgins had ordered him away from the apartment complex. He had to see Eva. He had to finish what he'd started last night. He had to tell her two things. One, he'd lied to her and two, that he was in love with her.

But when he got to her apartment, her Jeep wasn't in the parking lot, and she didn't answer her door. He retuned to his car and just as he reached for his cell phone to call her, the phone rang.

Rogers's number was on the caller ID.

"Hello?"

"We've got trouble."

"What is it?"

"Barksdale hacked you."

"What do you mean?"

"He's cloned your phone. He texted Eva St. George pretending to be you. It would show up on her caller ID as your number."

"What?"

"She's meeting him. Right now. Pier 16. Kilgore and I are across town, but we're on our way."

"Right." Adam hung up. He made a U-turn and headed for the beach.

Sure enough, Eva's yellow Jeep was parked in the lot.

He parked beside the Jeep and jumped out. To his left was a group sitting around a bonfire. There were several couples canoodling together in other spots scattered about. And then far off to his right, he saw a woman walking alone in the dark, a wooden pier looming in the darkness.

Eva.

He couldn't tell for sure if it was her or not, but he took off after her, following his gut.

She went down the cement staircase leading to underneath the pier. His pulse revved. After last night, he was instantly on alert. He quickened his pace. He would have called out her name, but the wind would have just snatched it and flung it out to sea.

Instead, he concentrated all his energy on running full out after her. It seemed like it took an hour, but was probably only a couple of minutes. His foot was on the last step of the cement staircase when he heard a soft feminine gasp, saw furtive movement in the shadows.

He drew his gun. He wasn't being caught unarmed tonight.

There were sounds of a struggle, as if someone was being dragged and he started running in the direction of the altercation.

"Eva!" he shouted, panic seizing him.

A muffled scream rent the air. The clouds parted like a curtain unveiling the moon and he could see everything in the brief splash of yellow light. A man was yanking Eva into the water.

Barksdale!

Even though he couldn't really see the man's face, he knew it was Barksdale as surely as he knew his own name. Was the bastard intent on drowning her?

That was when he saw the boat anchored just off shore. Barksdale was using a boat as a getaway vehicle.

Why hadn't he anticipated that? Why hadn't Higgins anticipated it?

Feeling like a wretched fool, he raced toward the end of the pier where Barksdale was already throwing a struggling Eva into the boat. The moon came out from behind a cloud again and he saw Barksdale raise his hand with something in it.

Moonlight reflected off metal.

A gun.

The chilled blood that had been sluggishly pumping through Adam's veins froze to ice. Barksdale was going to shoot Eva!

But instead of shooting her, Barksdale brought the butt of the gun down on Eva's head. She stopped struggling, and went limp in his arms.

Adam still wasn't close enough to fire off a shot. He ran as fast as he could, heart slamming into his rib cage, shoes kicking up sand that seemed to reach out, grab hold of him and yank him back.

"Stop!" he shouted. "Special Agent ONI."

Right. Like Barksdale was really going to stop what he was doing, raise his hands over his head and surrender on the spot.

But it was protocol. Adam wasn't going to give any scuzzball lawyer an excuse to spring Barksdale on a technicality. He'd make sure the bastard went to prison if it was the last thing he did.

Barksdale jerked on the throttle of the speedboat. Eva was draped lifelessly over the passenger seat.

If Adam hoped to save her, he had to do something now. He should call Kilgore and Rogers, but there wasn't time. He had to act. Protocol be damned. Frantically, he searched the beach.

What to do? What to do?

He heard salvation first before he spied it. A Jet Ski was pulling up to the pier.

Adam ran through the water, splashing and shouting, his gun in his hand. Startled, the man driving the Jet Ski fell off into the water and the engine died. Automatic kill switch.

The man raised his hands in front of his face, and sank back into the ocean. "Don't shoot, please don't shoot. I'm getting married in a week."

"I'm commandeering this craft in the name of the U.S. government," Adam said, stopping just long enough to snatch the key from the band around the guy's wrist. He stuffed his gun back into his shoulder holster, swung astride the Jet Ski and spun around, heading into the ocean.

Barksdale's boat had several yards on him, but the Jet Ski was souped-up with an extra powerful engine. He pushed it to full throttle and blasted into the darkness, pummeling oncoming waves. As he closed the distance between them, his hopes soared. He was going to catch up with them! He was going to save Eva.

Then Barksdale started firing at him.

THE BLAST ROUSED EVA.

Firecrackers? Who was shooting firecrackers?

Her head throbbed. She put a hand to her temple, felt something warm and sticky tracking down her skin. She was bleeding. Groggily, she blinked, trying to process what was happening.

Boat. She was in a boat on the ocean.

Keith, looking like a madman with wind-tousled hair

and frantic eyes, was at the helm. He had a gun and he kept turning around to fire at someone behind them.

She shook her head, trying to dislodge the lethargy that loosened her limbs.

In the darkness, she saw the small headlamp of a Jet Ski behind them.

Adam?

Hope expanded her heart. But why would Adam be on a Jet Ski chasing after them? She was hoping for a hero rescue from an accountant. That wasn't going to happen. It had to be someone else. Military police perhaps. NCIS. But why would the police be on a Jet Ski and not in a speedboat? It didn't make any sense.

Maybe Keith was just firing warning shots at someone who'd gotten too close. Probably no one was pursuing them at all. That thought shriveled her budding hope. If she wanted out of this, she was going to have to save herself. She'd learned a long time ago you couldn't depend on anyone else to rescue you.

"What are you doing?" she demanded.

Keith whipped his head around. "I'm kidnapping you."

That stunned her. "What for?"

"You haven't figured it out? Are you really that stupid? I knew you were an airhead, but I didn't think you were totally clueless."

She couldn't see his face very well in the darkness, but he was mocking her with an arrogant snarl. "Figured out what?"

"Give me the locket."

She reached up to finger the chain of the locket. "Sure. Fine."

"Shit," Keith said, and pushed the throttle on the boat

as fast as it would go. It felt like warp speed as they zoomed through the night.

Eva whipped her head around to see the Jet Ski gaining ground. A fresh flicker of hope flared in the embers of disappointment and fear. "Who's following us?"

"Not sure, but I'm presuming it's your boyfriend."

"Adam?"

"You got more than one boyfriend?" Barksdale stuffed the gun in his waistband and held out his right palm as he kept his left hand on the steering wheel. "Give me the locket."

This was her chance to act. He'd tucked the gun away. All she had to do was run at him, slam into him with her shoulders, and knock him overboard. She bent her knees and sprung up. Her head spun dizzily and her wobbly legs collapsed. She fell back against the seat.

Keith laughed, reached over, twisted his fingers around the chain of the locket and yanked it off her neck. Pieces of the delicate platinum chain scattered in the darkness.

"Stupid bitch, I don't give a damn about the locket. I want what's inside." He jammed the locket in his pocket, then took hold of the gun again.

"What's inside?"

"My ticket to freedom."

She was trembling all over. From the cold, from fear of Keith's gun, from the realization that she had stepped into deep water and was in way over her head. "Why would Adam be following us?"

Keith paused a moment to wave the gun in her face as a threat, then turned to shoot at the Jet Ski. "He's ONI."

"Office of Naval Intelligence?"

"Ding, ding, ding, Johnny," he said in a voice like a

game show announcer. "Tell Ms. St. George what she's won. Could it be a one-way ticket to the bottom of the ocean?"

Eva's face went icy. Keith was going to kill her. "But why? What did I do?"

"You got caught up in our little game of cat and mouse."

"Whose game?"

"Mine and Mancuso's."

"Will you just stop talking in circles and tell me what you're talking about? You're going to kill me anyway and I deserve to know why I'm going to die."

"I don't have to tell you shit." He pressed the hot gun against her cold forehead. The acrid smell of gunpowder filled her nose.

Terrified, Eva shrank back against the seat, palms raised. "Okay, okay."

He pulled the gun away to shoot into the darkness again. Gunfire was so damned loud. "But, since you asked so nicely, yeah, okay, I'll clue you in. Otherwise you'll never figure it out."

"Figure what out?"

"You take people at face value which is a very stupid thing to do, by the way. Everyone lies."

"Yes, yes, I'm a stupid idiot for trusting people, for liking you."

"You liked me only because I'm good at making people like me when I need to be. People are such damned sheep. They see what they want to see, believe what they want to believe."

That was true enough of her. She felt so wretchedly stupid. Keith was right. She was blind and dumb and trusting. Far too trusting. She'd trusted Adam as well and apparently he wasn't what he seemed, either.

But right now, she took a great deal of comfort in the fact that he was a naval intelligence officer and not an accountant.

"What is this all about, Keith? What have I gotten wrapped up in?"

"Prototype military weapons."

"You stole your country's secrets? For what? To sell to the highest bidder? You're a traitor as well as a thief."

"Sticks and stones." Keith fired the gun again and Eva cringed. "Dammit. Time to reload."

He set the gun on the seat, and dug in his pocket for a new clip. Eva thought again about attacking him or going for the empty gun and throwing it overboard, but Keith wagged his finger at her. "No, no."

He jammed the clip into the gun one-handed and turned to fire another shot.

She slapped her hands over her ears. The Jet Ski was still behind them. Adam was coming to save her. She just had to hold on a little while longer, keep Keith talking.

"So how did you steal top secret documents?"

"Your boyfriend was working on encrypting the documents. He thought he was so good, such the little rule follower. He had no clue I'd managed to hack into his system until after I'd already stolen the information right out from under his nose."

"How did you manage to do that?"

He leaned over to caress her cheek with the nose of the gun.

Eva shuddered. One careless move and the gun could go off. Kill her dead.

He's going to kill you anyway.

The reality of the situation finally hit her. She was going to die without ever telling Adam she loved him.

But did she really love him? She thought she did, but that was before she found out he'd been lying to her. She didn't even know who he really was.

"If I told you, I'd have to kill you." Barksdale chortled. "Wait, I *am* going to kill you, so I might as well tell you. Besides, if it wasn't for you, none of this would have been possible."

"What?" Eva blinked, pulling her mind from thoughts of Adam and focusing on Keith. She had to be present and fully alert if she had any hopes of getting out of this alive.

"You're the one who led me to the people who're going to pay me six million dollars for what's inside your locket."

"What are you talking about?"

"Why did you think I dated you?"

"I thought you liked me."

"Well, you do have one hell of a body, I'll give you that." Keith's eyes raked over her breasts. "But no, I cozied up to you because of your class."

"What's that got to do with anything?"

He proceeded to explain how his civilian job with the ONI had put him in the position to access foreign nationals on the government watch list. "When I found one that had influential connections in a wealthy country willing to pay for the secrets I could provide, I couldn't really approach him and say, 'Hi, my name's Keith, I want to steal U.S. secrets for your government.' He would have thought I was trying to set him up. Then I discovered he took yoga at your studio. It seemed the perfect opportunity. Take a few classes. Befriend you. Get you to introduce me, then drop a few hints until he approached me with an offer."

"You used me."

"Wake up, princess. You were a means to an end. That's all you ever were. A foil."

That hit her hard. Why hadn't she suspected anything? Was she truly that damned gullible? That trusting? Clearly she was.

"How did you pull all this off?"

Keith looked proud of himself. "I'm an inventive guy."

"And yet, you didn't get away with it. The ONI is after you."

"Yes. Well, it was unfortunate that I didn't get more time to pass the microchip to my contact."

"The locket," she said as everything finally clicked. "That's why you gave it to me. You hid the microchip in it."

"After I downloaded the data onto the microchip I realized they were already on to me. I left the base, but I was afraid I was being followed. I didn't know if they were going to arrest me right then or wait to see if I went to my contact. I was sitting at a stoplight, saw the jewelry store and it all fell into place. I pulled over, went in, bought the locket—which by the way, has a secret compartment, just perfect for hiding a microchip. I drove to the yoga studio, gave you the locket and just as I was leaving, they arrested me. They kept me for twenty-four hours, but didn't have enough evidence to hold me."

"That's when you came back to the studio, broke up with me and asked for the locket back."

"I would already be out of the country by now if NCIS hadn't shown up when they did," he said. "By then the heat was on. They installed your boyfriend in the apartment across the street to watch your place and they put another ONI agent in your yoga class."

It all made sense now. She'd thought Adam had been

watching her because he was attracted to her. But he'd simply been spying on her, hoping she'd lead him to Keith. He wasn't following her now to save her. He was trying to arrest Keith. None of this had ever been about her. He'd only been doing his job and she was collateral fallout. He didn't care about her. He didn't love her.

A feeling so utterly wretched it was indescribable settled over her. Keith might as well kill her. She had nothing to live for.

"That's why you came to talk to me when I was out surfing," she said softly.

"Yeah, but I didn't know how to ask you about the locket without making you curious. I couldn't afford to have you snooping inside of it."

"And you're the one who texted me and said to meet you at the pier tonight, wearing the locket. It wasn't Adam."

"I cloned his phone." Keith gave a maniacal laugh. "I stole his file, cloned his phone—who's better than the ONI? And you fell for it. Dumb blonde to the bone."

A strangled sob escaped her throat.

"Ah, you're just now realizing the truth, aren't you? Poor baby. That bastard Mancuso used you just like I did. He broke your little Pollyanna heart."

She'd had enough of this. With a roar of anger, Eva gathered all her strength and lunged at him, going for his eyes with her fingers, gouging and poking.

"Bitch!" he screamed as she knocked him off balance. The gun flew from his hand, skittering across the floor of the boat.

Simultaneously, they dove for it, struggling and grappling.

With no one at the helm, the boat charged the waves

in a crazed bucking bronco dash, then sputtered and slowed from lack of gas.

They rolled. Keith punched her on the jaw.

Frick! That hurt.

He grabbed hold of the gun, then kicked her in the ribs. She absorbed the blow through gritted teeth. He was panting hard. "On your feet," he commanded.

She staggered to her knees, and used the seat to drag herself to a standing position. From the corner of her eye, she saw a light in the distance near international waters. Another boat? Had this been Keith's destination all along? A rendezvous with his buyer?

Behind them, the Jet Ski lagged, the small engine overpowered by the heavier waves this far out at sea.

"Okay," Keith said. "I've got what I came for. I've had enough of you." He racked the gun. "Party's over."

Eva closed her eyes. Held her breath. This was it.

She was going to die.

And her last thoughts were of Adam.

18

ADAM WAS CLOSE ENOUGH to see the body go into the water.

Emotion slammed into him, a cement truck of fear and pain, heartache and desperation. No. *No!*

Barksdale had thrown Eva overboard. Alive? Or had he shot her first?

Please, God, he prayed. *Please let her be alive.*

Refusing to entertain any other thought, he urged the Jet Ski forward.

Barksdale had turned the speedboat and headed toward a yacht anchored in international waters. He could go after Barksdale. Or he could go after Eva, save her from the water.

Eva was a good swimmer and she knew the ocean. If she was dead, she was dead. If she was alive, she could make it until he got back to her or until one of his team could rescue her.

That choice made sense. It was the smart thing to do. It's what Higgins would order him to do.

But Adam had learned that blindly following orders was not always the right thing to do. He had to follow his heart and if it cost him his career, well then so be it. It wasn't a choice. No contest.

He let Barksdale slip away, hopped the Jet Ski over a high wave and went in search of the woman he loved.

EVA CAME UP SPUTTERING, spitting out mouthfuls of salty ocean. Her eyes burned. She was dazed from the blow to the head, the things she'd learned tonight and frantically treading water, but she was still breathing.

What now? She heard nothing but the waves. Saw nothing but the black sky stretched above with a sprinkling of winking stars. She was a very long way from shore. Where was the Jet Ski? Did Adam have a clue she'd been thrown into the water? Or was he at this moment still pursuing Keith?

She rolled onto her back and floated for what felt like a very long time, but was probably only minutes.

A thin pencil of light cut through the darkness. Then she heard the Jet Ski. The engine died suddenly, but the headlamp stayed on.

"Eva!"

It was Adam, calling to her, a heavenly voice in the darkest of night.

"Adam," she croaked, surprised to hear her voice come out low and scratchy.

"Eva?"

"Here," she tried to shout, but she couldn't. "I'm here."

The Jet Ski engine revved up, the light drew closer. She waved a hand. "Here, here, I'm here."

Then miraculously, there he was, right in front of her. He cut the engine again, reached for her and his strong arms going around her tightly, pulling her up onto the Jet Ski amidst the buffeting waves.

"Adam," she whispered, "I..."

"Shh, don't talk now. Save your energy." He kissed her tenderly on the forehead, tucked her arms around his waist, started the Jet Ski and headed back to shore.

THEY REACHED THE BEACH some twenty minutes later. Commander Higgins and his team were waiting for him at a makeshift command post they'd set up. A Navy helicopter was in the air, flying out across the ocean. Eva had ridden with her face buried against his back, her arms wrapped tightly around his waist. Nothing had every felt so good, so wonderful. The woman he loved was alive. She'd survived.

"Mancuso," Higgins barked, the minute he docked the Jet Ski on the sand. "A word."

Rogers had a blanket. He wrapped it around Eva's shoulders.

"I'll be right back," Adam whispered, and then allowed Rogers to lead her away to an awaiting medic.

"Barksdale?" Higgins asked, hands on his hips.

Adam shook his head, and then explained what had happened. Told Higgins of his choice to save Eva instead of going after Barksdale. As soon as the words were out of his mouth, he knew by the expression on his commander's face that his career in the ONI was over. How could he blame Higgins? Because of Adam, highly classified government secrets had fallen into enemy hands.

He'd let down his country in the worst way possible.

"We can't touch him in international waters," Higgins said.

"I know, sir." He stood at attention. "What about the buyer? Did you apprehend him at the airport?"

"It was a red herring. The buyer is on the yacht. He planned on heading back to his country tonight. This was Barksdale's last chance. Looks like he made it."

"I have no excuse, sir," Adam says. "The fault is entirely mine. I assume from the message he sent Miss St. George via my cloned phone, that the microchip was in her locket. He must have been the one who tried to mug us last night and take the locket at that time."

"Did you ask Miss St. George if by some chance, he didn't get hold of the locket?"

"No, but—"

"Let's go ask her," Higgins interrupted. Obviously, the man was grasping at straws. The microchip was the only reason Barksdale had lured Eva to the beach. When he'd gotten his hands on her, he'd taken the locket.

Commander Higgins strode over to where the medic was checking Eva's blood pressure as she sat in the back of the ambulance. He introduced himself to Eva, and then asked, "Did Barksdale take your locket?"

"He did." Eva nodded.

Higgins swore, turning away.

"But," she said, "it wasn't the locket he gave me."

"Excuse me?" Higgins whirled back to her.

A saucy smile lifted her lips. That saucy smile Adam loved so much.

"I wasn't wearing the locket that Keith had given me. A locket's a pretty common piece of jewelry—I already had a cheap one." She shrugged. "Hell, I wouldn't be surprised if that's where Keith subconsciously got his idea for a hiding place—I wore it on a few dates. And remember, I thought I was going to meet Adam. I didn't realize Keith had cloned Adam's phone number and sent the message. After we had nearly gotten mugged over the necklace last night, I decided to wear the cheap one instead," she explained. "I couldn't imagine Adam would care."

Was he hearing this correctly? Barksdale hadn't gotten hold of the microchip after all? Adam fisted his hands, not really daring to hope.

Eva continued, "I tried to use Keith's ego to buy time for Adam to catch up to us. He was so distracted bragging about his own brilliance, he didn't realize it wasn't the same locket."

"So you still have the real locket?" Higgins asked.

"I do. It's back at my apartment."

"What are we waiting for?" Higgins said. "Let's go get it."

They arrived at Eva's apartment a few minutes later. She went into her bedroom, came out with the locket. She presented it to Higgins.

All three of them held their collective breaths as Higgins opened the locket. It was empty.

Disappointment shattered the hopes that had been building.

"Nothing," Higgins said.

"Keith said there's a secret compartment in the locket," Eva pointed out.

Higgins examined the locket closer. "By damn there is a little latch here. You got a multitool on you, Mancuso?"

Adam produced a multitool from his pocket, passing it to his boss. He slipped a glance over at Eva. She was watching him but he couldn't read the expression on her face. When their eyes met, she quickly looked away.

Higgins jiggled the pick in the locket and the secret compartment sprang open.

"Son of a bitch," he swore joyfully, and displayed the black microchip—not much bigger than a grain of rice—on the top of his index finger.

"That's what all the fuss was about?" Eva asked. "That tiny little thing?"

"Lady, this tiny little thing could have caused the U.S. some major trouble. Thanks to you and your smart thinking, disaster has been averted."

"It was Adam's idea," she said.

"Pardon?"

"He's the one who told me rich people wear duplicates of their fancy jewelry when they're in dicey situations. If it hadn't been for him, Keith would have gotten away with this."

Commander Higgins shot a speculative look Adam's way. "I'm getting this back to the ONI right away. Mancuso, I believe you deserve some leave time." He inclined his head toward Eva. "It's effective immediately."

"Yes, sir."

Commander Higgins left with the microchip. They went to change into dry clothes and met again in Eva's living room.

Adam opened his mouth to tell her how much he appreciated her, how happy he was that she'd survived, how proud he was of her, but she jumped in first, cutting him off.

"You lied to me," Eva's blue eyes narrowed to slits. "I trusted you and you lied to me."

The expression on her face tore him up inside. He put a hand out to touch her shoulder. "I'm sorry. It was my job."

She yanked away from him, her bottom lip trembling.

She blinked. "No. You don't get to blame it on your job. You lied to me."

"Yes," he admitted. "I lied to you, but—" He broke off.

She was right. He was making excuses. His mistake wasn't in keeping his identity a secret. That had been his assignment. No, where his sin had come in was in losing his head, breaking his own rules and following his heart. He should not have gotten involved with her on a personal level, not while she was his target. He should not have made love to her. If he'd stayed in his apartment and simply watched as he'd been assigned, he would never have hurt her.

"Eva," he said, stalling as he searched for the words he needed to apologize. He wasn't a man who apologized easily. He wasn't usually wrong. But he'd screwed up big-time. He'd hurt her. How he regretted hurting her.

"I think it's best if you left now." She turned her back to him, staring out the window. She looked so incredibly sad, so breakable.

"Sunshine, I—"

She crossed her arms over her chest. "Please, Adam, just leave. Don't make this goodbye any harder than it has to be."

Adam had had enough. He wasn't going to let her push him away. He had to try and make amends, had to make her see how much he loved her.

Love.

There it was. The word he'd been barely able to think, much less say. All along he'd been falling in love with her. Probably from the very first minute he watched her doing naked yoga. He thought of all they'd shared.

The long talks, the walks on the beach, surfing, golf. He thought of all the things they could share. The Sunday morning paper. Chicken soup when they were sick. Thanksgiving. Christmas. A home. A family.

His gut tightened. He wanted all that with her. Wanted her to be the mother of his kids. Wanted to love her for the rest of his days. "I can't leave until you at least hear me out."

She sighed, dropped her arms and turned to look at him. "You have five minutes starting now."

"I'm so damned sorry I lied to you. The last thing I ever wanted was to hurt you. I shouldn't have gotten involved with you. I put my mission in jeopardy, put your life at risk."

"It's true then, you regret getting involved with me?" She raised her stubborn little chin.

This was a no-win situation. The hope he'd been clinging to slid away. She wasn't going to forgive him, but he wasn't going down without a fight. He might be a lot of things, but he wasn't a quitter.

"I don't regret making love to you. Not for one second." He growled. "What I regret is the timing. I shouldn't have made love to you while you were under my protection."

"I never asked for your protection."

"No," he agreed, "you got caught in the back draft of our investigation of Barksdale."

"Admit it. You hold the fact that I was involved with Keith against me."

That chapped him. "I do not!"

"You think I follow my heart too easily. That I go for flash over substance. That I let a pretty face keep me from seeing what kind of person Keith was beneath it."

"That isn't my judgment of you."

Her nostrils flared. "Isn't it?"

"No. Never. It's your own judgment of yourself."

Eva's eyes widened and he could see that she finally got it. Her big heart was never the problem. What kept tripping her up was her own self-judgment.

"You're trying to be something you're not," he said. "Perhaps it's a backlash against your mother. You don't want to be like her. I get that. But having an open heart is a wonderful thing, Eva. It's what I love most about you."

"Love?" she whispered.

"Yes, dammit, love."

She was trembling all over, her knees quaking. "What are you saying, Adam?"

"I'm saying I'm in love with you, Eva St. George. It's only been a couple of weeks, but I've fallen in love. I'm saying that while it was my assignment to watch and catch Barksdale if he showed up, I violated my ethics and allowed myself to get involved. Your open heart opened my heart. Before you came into my life I never knew I could feel this way. I heard people talk about love but—other than the love I feel for my family—I didn't get what all the fuss was about. I never understood how someone could come into your life and steal away a piece of your heart forever."

A smile tipped her lips and tears misted her eyes. "You're saying I stole your heart?"

"Took it right out from under my nose."

"Adam," she said his name on a sigh.

He reached for her then and this time, she didn't pull away. He tugged her into his embrace. "Forgive me, for being a dumb ass."

"You're forgiven."

He dipped his head, peered deeply into her eyes. "You

rock my world, Eva. Before I met you, I thought I was the best I could be. Living up to a moral code, being a good investigator, toeing the line, following orders."

"You *are* pretty awesome."

"Not as awesome as you are, Sunshine. You showed me how shut down I really was. How I was hiding behind my principles because I didn't want to face the truth."

"What truth is that?"

"That I'd become inflexible and uncompromising. That I was so determined not to let my heart rule my head that I almost missed the best thing that ever happened to me."

"And what would that be?"

"You." He tightened his grip around her. "Until you, I'd never felt like this."

"Like what?"

"Shout-it-from-the-mountain-top exhilarated. It's like the sun finally came out after a month of rain. It's like I was Rip van Winkle and I just woke up and the world looks amazing and brand-new and full of possibilities and it's all because of you."

"Me?" Her voice sounded high and reedy, as if she didn't quite believe him.

"You," he confirmed, and put both hands on her shoulders.

"Just shut up and kiss me," she said.

"Is that an order?"

"Yes."

"I try never to disobey orders."

"Good for y—"

He kissed her hard and long. Showing her with his lips just how much he wanted and needed her. Communicating in the best way he knew how, with action instead of words.

She kissed him back with equal fervor, giving as good as she got, matching his tongue stroke for stroke, taking him to the clouds with her, his spontaneous, free-spirited woman.

The heat of their bodies scorched him to his soul. He wanted her, needed her. Not just for now, but forever.

"Adam," she murmured against his lips. "Adam."

"Eva."

They kissed, wind swirling the curtains around the open window.

"So," he said, pulling back and wriggling his eyebrows. "My place or yours?"

Eva cast a glance around. "I know the perfect spot on the beach. We could slip behind a sand dune..."

"Are you suggesting we break all the rules?"

"You broke all the rules to get me, right?"

"Right."

She grinned wickedly, touched the tip of her tongue to her upper lip, took him by the hand and led him to his salvation.

ADAM SETTLED HER ON HER BACK in the sand, underneath the palm trees. The sound of the surf pounded in her ears, but it couldn't drown out the sound of her beating heart. Beating it seemed, just for him. His palms caressed her arms, tracing over the thin silk of the blouse she had on.

She needed him. Needed him so badly she ached to her bones. Without him, she was incomplete, only one half of a whole.

And her need was far more than physical. She loved him. Wanted him. For now. Forever. It was scary this need. She shouldn't love him this much. It was dangerous. If it all went away tomorrow, she'd be left a broken woman.

"Don't look so worried," he murmured, and pressed his lips to her brow. "Being loved is a good thing. A grand thing. The best damned thing of all."

"I've never been in love before. You're my first. The first man I've ever loved." Once the words were said out loud, she felt them to the depths of her soul.

"You're mine, Eva St. George," he whispered. "You're mine and I'm yours. Remember that always."

They gazed into each other's eyes. His shirt was off, hers unbuttoned. All control evaporated. Frenzied, they finished undressing each other, leaving their clothes strewn about the sand.

He positioned himself over her, resting his weight on his forearms and looked down into her face. She smiled up at him. He was so incredibly handsome. Her man.

Her man.

She said the words in her head, unafraid and happy.

He kneed her thighs apart and she opened her legs, letting him in.

Adam made a masculine sound of pure pleasure and sank into her deep and sweet. His eyes glowed hot, his thrusts long, hard and slow. He captured her lips, roughly, but lovingly. Their mouths clung as he increased the tempo of their mating.

"I love you," she whispered fiercely, "more than anyone or anything I have ever known."

"More than yoga?"

"Much more."

"More than surfing?"

"Yes, yes."

He moved purposefully, the rhythm easy and languid.

She whimpered and pressed against him, urging him to pick up the pace, but he only laughed and went even slower. Tension built.

Eva was acutely aware of every breath, every pulse. He cupped her buttocks as he slid in and out, in and out, the ocean tide, building to a crest.

His hands pulled her helplessly against him. Rocking. Rocking. A soft moan escaped her throat, slipped into the night to mingle with his noises. His mouth burned hers, hot and erotic, tender and loving, but he never lost the rhythm. Their bodies were joined, fused, perfectly matched. Each movement elicited more delight, more surprise.

Higher and higher he drove her. The light of love was in his eyes, real and true and forever. She smiled at him and he laughed a laugh that hugged her soul.

At the peak, she cried his name, a chant, a litany, a deep-throated mantra. "Adam, Adam, Adam."

His body tensed and she wrapped her legs around his waist, pulling him in as deep as he could go. Release claimed them both in that instance and he followed right with her, dropping into the abyss, free-falling into the sensuous undertow, going under and loving every minute of it. Drowning. Lost. And yet at the same time utterly found.

Spent, he collapsed against her, burying his face in the hollow of her neck.

She drew in the scent of him, breathed deep.

They clung to each other, quivering with sensation, inhaling this new life together. Adam stroked her, murmured sweet nothings until her heart rate returned to normal and her body had stilled.

"Sunshine," he whispered. "You've saved me from myself."

Eva smiled into the darkness, knowing the truth was that they'd saved each other.

Epilogue

COMMANDER HIGGINS AND HIS TEAM found Keith Barksdale floating in the ocean on a pitiful life preserver two days later, dehydrated and delirious. He was lucky his associates hadn't seen fit to put a bullet in his head when he'd been unable to produce the promised microchip. They arrested him on a grocery list of charges, primarily attempted treason.

Even though he was on leave, Adam had gone to the base to look Barksdale in the eyes. He wanted to see for himself what kind of man would try to sell out his country to pay off gambling debts. He was surprised at how ordinary Barksdale looked.

After that, he went to meet Eva at Shady Palms Country Club where they had a noon tee time.

"How'd it go?" she asked, looking as though she'd been golfing there all her life in that cute pink golfing outfit and the clubs he'd bought her.

"He's looking at some stiff charges."

"I can't believe I was so easy fooled." She shook her head.

"Don't beat yourself up over it. Barksdale is a master at fooling people. But it's all over now. He's in custody and we can put the past behind us." He took her arm and helped her into the golf cart.

They hadn't had a chance to talk about their future. There hadn't been much time for it yet. But Adam was the happiest he'd ever been. He wanted to bring it up, but didn't really know where to begin. He leaned over to kiss her, felt a shiver of delight run over her body.

"Adam, that's bold. You kissing me in public."

"Hey, you loosened me up." He kissed her again. How he loved his sweet, spontaneous, sunny woman.

"Well, don't get too loose. Your reserve is part of your charm."

"It is?"

"You're the one who's supposed to keep me grounded, remember."

"Yes, ma'am." He chuckled and guided the golf cart toward the first hole. "You know, I was thinking it might be a good time for you to meet my parents."

Eva blinked. "Really?"

"They're right over there." He pointed to an older couple waiting for them at the tee.

"Oh my, oh gosh. I can't believe you sprung this on me." Eva sucked in her breath.

"When I called them and told them I'd found the woman I wanted to spend my life with, they insisted on meeting you. They know when I say something I mean it."

"Adam," she whispered. "Is this a proposal?"

"Not yet. I'm going to do that up right, but we're getting there."

Eva's heart fluttered. She was so nervous. What were his parents going to think of her? His father was a senator for heavens sake.

But she worried for no reason. The minute they

stepped from the golf cart, Adam's mother enveloped her in a big hug and his father shook her hand. They were so warm and welcoming, she instantly felt at home.

And when the round of golf was over and they were all headed to the country club café for lunch, Adam slung his arm around her, smiling at his folks. "What did I tell you, Mom and Dad. I know a good thing when I see her."

And as his parents walked ahead of them out of earshot, he leaned down to whisper, "Doing naked yoga."

"Voyeur," she whispered back.

"Exhibitionist."

"Spy." She giggled.

"Target."

"Are you as turned-on as I am?"

"More," he said, and then called out to his parents, "Mom, Dad, we'll catch up with you at dinner. We forgot there's somewhere else we have to be."

Laughing together, they raced to her Jeep, drove back to that secluded beach and proceeded to break all the rules all over again.

* * * * *

COMING NEXT MONTH

Available May 31, 2011

#615 REAL MEN WEAR PLAID!
Encounters
Rhonda Nelson

#616 TERMS OF SURRENDER
Uniformly Hot!
Leslie Kelly

#617 RECKLESS PLEASURES
The Pleasure Seekers
Tori Carrington

#618 SHOULD'VE BEEN A COWBOY
Sons of Chance
Vicki Lewis Thompson

#619 HOT TO THE TOUCH
Checking E-Males
Isabel Sharpe

#620 MINE UNTIL MORNING
24 Hours: Blackout
Samantha Hunter

HBCNM0511

REQUEST YOUR FREE BOOKS!
2 FREE NOVELS PLUS 2 FREE GIFTS!

red-hot reads!

YES! Please send me 2 FREE Harlequin® Blaze® novels and my 2 FREE gifts (gifts are worth about $10). After receiving them, if I don't wish to receive any more books, I can return the shipping statement marked "cancel." If I don't cancel, I will receive 6 brand-new novels every month and be billed just $4.24 per book in the U.S. or $4.71 per book in Canada. That's a saving of at least 15% off the cover price. It's quite a bargain. Shipping and handling is just 50¢ per book in the U.S. and 75¢ per book in Canada.* I understand that accepting the 2 free books and gifts places me under no obligation to buy anything. I can always return a shipment and cancel at any time. Even if I never buy another book, the two free books and gifts are mine to keep forever.

151/351 HDN FC4T

Name	(PLEASE PRINT)	

Address		Apt. #

City	State/Prov.	Zip/Postal Code

Signature (if under 18, a parent or guardian must sign)

Mail to the **Reader Service:**
IN U.S.A.: P.O. Box 1867, Buffalo, NY 14240-1867
IN CANADA: P.O. Box 609, Fort Erie, Ontario L2A 5X3

Not valid for current subscribers to Harlequin Blaze books.

Want to try two free books from another line?
Call 1-800-873-8635 or visit www.ReaderService.com.

* Terms and prices subject to change without notice. Prices do not include applicable taxes. Sales tax applicable in N.Y. Canadian residents will be charged applicable taxes. Offer not valid in Quebec. This offer is limited to one order per household. All orders subject to credit approval. Credit or debit balances in a customer's account(s) may be offset by any other outstanding balance owed by or to the customer. Please allow 4 to 6 weeks for delivery. Offer available while quantities last.

Your Privacy—The Reader Service is committed to protecting your privacy. Our Privacy Policy is available online at www.ReaderService.com or upon request from the Reader Service.

We make a portion of our mailing list available to reputable third parties that offer products we believe may interest you. If you prefer that we not exchange your name with third parties, or if you wish to clarify or modify your communication preferences, please visit us at www.ReaderService.com/consumerschoice or write to us at Reader Service Preference Service, P.O. Box 9062, Buffalo, NY 14269. Include your complete name and address.

"THANKS FOR NOT TURNING ON THE LIGHTS," Tyler said. "I'm a mess."

"Not in my book." Even in low light, Alex had a good view of her yellow shirt plastered to her body. It was all he could do not to reach for her, mud and all. But the next move needed to be hers, not his.

She slicked her wet hair back and squeezed some water out of the ends as she glanced upward. "I like the sound of the rain on a tin roof."

"Me, too."

She met his gaze briefly and looked away. "Where's the sink?"

"At the far end, beyond the last stall."

Tyler's running shoes squished as she walked down the aisle between the rows of stalls. She glanced sideways at Alex. "So how much of a cowboy are you these days? Do you ride the range and stuff?"

"I ride." He liked being able to say that. "Why?"

"Just wondered. Last summer, you were still a city boy. You even told me you weren't the cowboy type, but you're...different now."

He wasn't sure if that was a good thing or a bad thing. Maybe she preferred city boys to cowboys. "How am I different?"

"Well, you dress differently, and your hair's a little longer. Your face seems a little more chiseled, but maybe that's because of your hair. Also, there's something else, something harder to define, an attitude…"

"Are you saying I have an attitude?"

"Not in a bad way. It's more like a quiet confidence."

He was flattered, but still he had to laugh. "I just admitted a while ago that I have all kinds of doubts about this event tomorrow. That doesn't seem like quiet confidence to me."

"This isn't about your job, it's about…your…" She took a deep breath. "It's about your sex appeal, okay? I have no business talking about it, because it will only make me want to do things I shouldn't do." She started toward the end of the barn. "Now, where's that sink? We need to get cleaned up and go back to the house. Dinner is probably ready, and I—"

He spun her around and pulled her into his arms, mud and all. "Let's do those things." Then he kissed her, knowing that she would kiss him back, knowing that this time he would take that kiss where he wanted it to go. And she would let him.

Follow Tyler and Alex's wild adventures in
SHOULD'VE BEEN A COWBOY
Available June 2011 only from Harlequin® Blaze™
wherever books are sold.

Harlequin® Blaze™
red-hot reads

Do you need a cowboy fix?

NEW YORK TIMES BESTSELLING AUTHOR

Vicki Lewis Thompson

RETURNS WITH HER SIZZLING TRILOGY…

Sons of Chance

Chance isn't just the last name of these rugged
Wyoming cowboys—it's their motto, too!

Take a chance…on a Chance!

Saddle up with:
SHOULD'VE BEEN A COWBOY (June)
COWBOY UP (July)
COWBOYS LIKE US (August)

Available from Harlequin® Blaze™
wherever books are sold.

www.eHarlequin.com

HB79622